The Painted Window

By G. H. Teed

Illustrated by Val Reading

First published in the Union Jack magazine,

24 March 1923.

Stillwoods Edition, 2020

Stillwoods.Blogspot.Ca

Catalogue Information:
Title: The Painted Window
Author: G. H. Teed (1886-1938)
Illustrated by: Val Reading
First published anonymously in the Union Jack magazine, Series 2, No. 1015, 24 March 1923.
This Edition: Stillwoods, 2020 (Doug Frizzle)
ISBN Canada 978-1-989788-20-2
Blog: Stillwoods.Blogspot.Ca
Author Blog: http://ghteed.blogspot.com/
Storefront: http://www.lulu.com/spotlight/lulubook22

Keywords: Sexton Blake, British fictional detective, Huxton Rymer, Singapore

A fine yarn, complete in this issue, of SEXTON BLAKE and HUXTON RYMER in SINGAPORE. Though complete in itself, it is also a sequel to "The Pearls of Benjemasin," which appeared last week (No. 1014) You can refresh your memory of the events that preceded these here narrated by reading what follows.

THOSE who read "The Case of the Pearls of Benjemasin" will recall that the wonderful pair of matched pink pearls, known as the Pearls of Benjemasin, were bought by an island trader of the Sulu Sea known as John Creek who, at a considerable risk, managed to get them through to Hong-Kong.

Here he intended submitting them to Sexton Blake for examination on behalf of the well-known Paris gem dealer, M. Acier.

Unknown to Creek, he was followed all the way from Benjemasin by an adventurer, who went under the name of Atwood.

In Benjemasin Atwood had originally had possession of the pearls, which he had taken from a man whom he had killed near Broome, in Western Australia.

He had disposed of them in Benjemasin to a Chinaman, one Hop Sing; and, on the night on which Hop Sing disposed of them to Creek, Atwood killed Hop Sing, thinking the Celestial still had the gems in

his possession.

Discovering the truth, he followed Creek to Manila, but there his money gave out. He managed, however, to secure passage by the ship Kui Sang as a stoker, and on this same ship John Creek and Dr. Huxton Rymer were travelling as passengers.

Rymer learned Atwood's secret, and decided to get possession of the pearls. By clever strategy, after the ship arrived in Hong-Kong, he succeeded in doing so.

Blake, who was at the Hong-Kong hotel, took the matter in hand, and turned the tables on Rymer, securing the pearls by the same strategy which Rymer had employed.

After that, Blake, who cannot spare the time which legal proceedings would entail, gives Rymer a warning, and advises him to clear out.

Atwood has been killed by Tong, vengeance for the murder of Hop Sing in Benjemasin. After completing the deal with John Creek, Blake and Tinker leave Hong-Kong by the Amiral Lebon, of a French line, and it is not until they are almost across to Saigon that they discover Rymer is a second-class passenger on the same steamer.

Blake is more amused than angry, for he knows Rymer has no chance of getting possession of the pearls from him, if that is his reason for travelling by the French boat.

However, both he and Tinker were due for further adventures owing to the pearls before they completed the voyage, as the story shows.

The Painted Window

A fine yarn, complete in this issue, of SEXTON BLAKE and HUXTON RYMER in SINGAPORE. Though complete in itself, it is also a sequel to "The Pearls of Benjemasin," which appeared last week. You can refresh your memory of the events that preceded those here narrated by reading :: :: what follows. :: ::

IT was Tinker, who had been prowling about the after-part of the Amiral Lebon, who made the surprising discovery that Dr. Huxton Rymer, whom they thought had been left behind in Hong-Kong, was a second-class passenger on the same ship.

Tinker had entered the small second-class smoking-saloon and then had stopped, mouth literally agape, at the sight of Rymer sitting at one of the tables and coolly playing double Canfield with one of the other passengers.

He had managed to control his amazement before Rymer looked up and saw him; but the adventurer did not appear in the least alarmed at being discovered.

He had nodded his head to Tinker, and then had proceeded with his play as if the meeting was just an ordinary shipboard incident. As for Tinker, he returned to the main promenade deck, where he found Blake ensconced in a rattan deck-chair, reading.

"What do you think, guv'nor?" asked Tinker, as he sat down, "Whom do you think is on board in the second-class?"

"Haven't an idea, my lad. Is it someone we know?"

"It is," responded Tinker. "It is Rymer."

Blake lowered his book and smiled.

"Rymer, eh? I am not altogether surprised. He had to get out of Hong-Kong by the quickest means, and I suppose this ship suited him better than any other.

"But I have reason to believe that he is at present well supplied with funds, and knowing Rymer's weakness for the best of everything, I am a little puzzled at his travelling second class.

"It is probable that he wishes to efface himself as much as possible, for he must have known that we were on board."

"What will you do, guv'nor? Will you say anything to the captain?"

"No; why should I? After all, he can't throw Rymer over the side; and unless Rymer makes some trouble on board —which he is not fool enough to do —the captain couldn't take any action.

"I presume he has paid his fare in the usual way; and besides, this is a French ship. No, my lad, as far as we are concerned, let him travel in peace.

"The Pearls of Benjemasin are quite safe in the ship's strong-room, so we have nothing to worry about. Nor is Rymer fool enough to attempt to start any sort of personal vendetta against us while we are on board."

"He certainly wasn't worried a bit when he caught sight of me," remarked Tinker, with a grin.

"He probably knew all along that we were on board, and knew the chances were we should discover him. Therefore, he was prepared for the meeting."

Blake returned to his book then, and Tinker walked to the rail, where he stood contemplating the sun-washed wastes of the China Sea.

Tinker was considerably intrigued at finding Rymer on board, and despite Blake's indifference, he determined to keep an eye on the adventurer.

But by the time they arrived at Saigon, Tinker had to confess that, despite all his efforts, results had been nil.

Rymer appeared to conduct himself just as any other passenger, and as far as Tinker could discover, had made no attempt to encroach on the first-class section of the ship. As for Blake, he had apparently dismissed the adventurer from his mind, for he scarcely referred to Rymer until they docked at Saigon.

There, however, he received a cablegram which once more brought Rymer's name up in the conversation. This cable was from M. Acier, the Paris gem merchant, for whom Blake had bought the Pearls of Benjemasin, and had been forwarded on from Hong-Kong in care of Captain Devantier of the Amiral Lebon by the ship's Hong-Kong agents.

The date of its receipt in Hong-Kong showed that it had been received the day after the Amiral Lebon had cleared. It ran as follows;

"Your cable received, note you intend proceeding Amiral Lebon to Colombo. If likely be delayed Colombo please hand over pearls and jade purchased my account to my agent Jean Pascal, who has been purchasing rubies my account in Burmah and who returns to France from Singapore by Amiral Lebon. If you are proceeding whole way by Lebon unnecessary hand over to Pascal. Hope you will find possible pass through Paris on way to London.—(Signed) ACIER."

At the time of receiving the telegram, Blake and Tinker had been standing on the main deck, up near the head of the first-class gangway, preparatory to going ashore.

As the Amiral Lebon would remain in Saigon for two days, it

2

was their intention to put up at the Hotel de l'Europe and motor out into the country back of Saigon. There, the magnificent highways made by the French are unsurpassed for smooth motoring and beauty of surroundings.

They wind for hundreds of kilometres between vivid rice fields, groves of slender areca palms, and then on into the dense timber of the higher country.

There was a considerable crowd jostling about the gangway, and in order to read the telegram, Blake had moved to the rail. Aft, another gangway had been thrown out for the second-class passengers, but owning to the crowd and their own preoccupation, neither Blake nor Tinker had seen their old enemy, Rymer, descend the gangway and pause on the dock to watch Blake as he received the cablegram and tore it open.

When he had read it, Blake handed it to Tinker, and when the lad had grasped the contents, Blake took it and tore it into several small pieces.

Glancing over the side, he saw that there was a width of about two feet of water between the side of the ship and the wharf, and although the Saigon River runs sluggishly there between its low banks, several small chips were making perceptible progress past the side.

Not that Blake considered any extraordinary precaution necessary in destroying the cablegram. Even if the thought of Rymer had occurred to him he would not have seen any cause for worry in that, for the pearls were quite safe in the ship's strong-room, and if he handed them over to M. Acier's agent in Singapore, he had no doubt that they would remain in the strong-room until the ship reached Marseilles.

His tearing up of the cablegram into small pieces and his preliminary glance over the side were both perfectly natural actions in one whose whole life was based on caution.

It came as second nature to Sexton Blake not to leave scraps of writing lying about. Therefore he had no idea that Rymer was watching him surreptitiously as he dropped the pieces over the side of the ship and turned to follow Tinker down the gangway.

He would have been highly interested, on reaching the dock, had he seen what was afoot farther along. But he did not see, for he and Tinker went with the other passengers towards the gates at the head of the wharf on their way to the hotel.

But had they gone in the other direction, they might have seen Huxton Rymer hasten across the wharf and catch a lounging coolie by the shoulder. He forcibly propelled the coolie back to the edge of the wharf, just above where Rymer could see the pieces of torn paper floating along.

He pointed them out to the coolie; then he took out a ten-dollar bill and showed it to the man.

For ten dollars all at once the average coolie would cheerfully commit murder, and the one whom Rymer had grasped was as eager to possess that ten-dollar note as any of his fellows would have been.

He went over the side of the wharf and into the water like an eel. He might have been greased, so smoothly did he slide through the water; and then, as he swam, he began collecting the bits of paper which the crazy white man seemed to want, putting the bits in his mouth while he searched for others.

Round and round he swam, while Rymer's eyes darted hither and thither. Then, when he could see no more bits of paper, he made a gesture, and the coolie swam to the wharf.

Rymer knelt down and gave him a hand. A few seconds later the torn paper and the ten-dollar note changed hands, and while the coolie stuffed the note into the folds of his loin-cloth and took to his heels to escape his "friends," Rymer went back up the gangway and down into his cabin to try and piece together the torn paper, and thus discover just what it was that had been cabled to Sexton Blake.

Not for a single moment did Rymer dream that the cable would bear any reference to the pearls which he had won and lost in Hong-Kong. Nor was it until more than an hour's patient work that he came upon the word.

But by that time he had managed to make quite a little progress with the jigsaw, and as the form grew slowly beneath his fingers, he worked more patiently than ever. In just under three hours from the time he had sent the coolie into the water, Huxton Rymer had completed the puzzle —all but two small bits, which must have gone out into the stream before the coolie could secure them.

He was perspiring profusely in the hot cabin, even though the fan was going, but he was content, for what he read in the cablegram he had succeeded in piecing together had determined him to continue on to Singapore, and not to leave the ship at Saigon as he had previously intended.

IT was a warm but quiet and uneventful run from Saigon down through the Gulf of Siam to Singapore. Just the day before they were due at the "crossroads of the East," Blake made his way to the second-class quarters. He found Rymer there, playing double Canfield in the smoking-saloon, just as Tinker had seen him some days before.

Blake waited until the game was over, then he signed to Rymer that he wished to speak to him. When they were out on deck where their conversation could not be overheard, Blake said:

"How far do you propose going by this steamer?"

"What has that to do with you?" asked Rymer curtly.

"Possibly nothing to do with me, but a great deal to do with you, Rymer. I want to give you a tip. Better leave the ship at Singapore. I do not think you would be wise to go on as far as Colombo."

"Why not?"

"Because I say so. I have said nothing about your coming this far, but I object to your going on to Colombo. If you do you will regret it."

"Well, it isn't any of your business; but I don't mind telling you that I had intended leaving at Singapore, anyway."

"That is all right, then. If you stick to that I shall not worry you. But if you try to make Colombo while I am in this part of the world you will regret it.

"What happened in Hong-Kong means nothing to me so long as you behave yourself. You tried to pull off something there, and I managed to best you at your own game. With me the incident is closed. It rests entirely with you whether I re-open it or not."

"You needn't worry!" snapped Rymer. "I have already told you that I intend leaving at Singapore. But if I wanted to go on to Colombo you wouldn't stop me!"

Blake shrugged.

"You try it, and see!" he said, and with that, stalked away.

When they docked at the Messageries Maritimes dock in Singapore, Blake and Tinker did not go ashore with the first rush of passengers.

As in Saigon, they were due to remain two days in port, during which time Blake and Tinker intended putting up at one of the hotels in the town. But first Blake wanted to wait and see if M. Acier's agent, Pascal, would put in an appearance.

As a matter of fact, the Frenchman came aboard very soon after they docked, and when he had found Blake, introduced himself. Blake led the way into the smoking-saloon, where the trio sat down at a table while Blake inspected the agent's credentials.

When he was satisfied that they were all in order, and had made a careful comparison of Pascal's features with the photograph on his passport and identity-card, he handed them back.

"Well, M. Pascal," he said pleasantly, "what do you wish me to do? I received a cablegram from M. Acier saying that you intended returning to France by this steamer, and if I should make a short stay in Colombo, he asked me to hand over to you certain purchases which I made for him in Hong-Kong. What are your intentions?"

"My plans have been altered, M. Blake, since I cabled to M. Acier informing him that I would sail from Singapore by the Amiral Lebon. I have received another cable from him, authorising me to carry out a suggestion which I made to him.

"I have reason believe that I may be able to sell the two pearls you have with you to one of the native princes in Malaya. I have made an appointment with this prince to meet him in Kuala Lumpur, and if the pearls are what he wants, I fancy I can make a deal with him.

"That all depends if they are what M. Acier has led me to think they are. In that case, I would not be able to sail by this steamer, but would have to wait for the Sphinx, which is due in a week's time."

"That means, then, that you want me to hand over the pearls in any case."

"Yes, if you will be so good."

"Certainly. But what about the jade? I bought some very choice bits of pink jade in Hong-Kong on M. Acier's account."

"Would you mind retaining that and handing it to M. Acier when you pass through Paris? I may tell you, in confidence, that I am already carrying a very valuable lot of rubies which I bought in Moulmein, and I do not wish to add to my responsibilities if I can help it."

"I have no objection to keeping the jade, M. Pascal. It is my intention to continue on to Colombo by this ship and tranship there to a Bibby boat, as I have some affairs to attend to in Colombo.

"I shall hand over the pearls to you today; but, before doing so, I expect you will not mind accompanying me to the French Consulate here just to secure further confirmation there of your credentials.

"I am not questioning you or them, but these two pearls are worth a very large amount, and we have already had quite a little excitement over them."

"I shall go to the consulate with pleasure, M. Blake. I, too, should prefer that you feel perfectly sure of me. I can quite understand your caution. It is what I would do myself. Do you mean to say that someone has tried to steal the pearls?"

Blake smiled grimly.

"Not only tried, but succeeded, M. Pascal. But that was before I made the purchase on behalf of M. Acier, and we have had no trouble since.

"At the same time, the man who did gain possession of them for a few hours was also a passenger with us down from Hong-Kong. If he dreamed for a single moment that the pearls were to be handed over to you here, you may rest assured that he would spare no effort to get hold of them."

"I will risk that," asserted the Frenchman confidently. "He will have to be clever to trick me."

"I wouldn't make the mistake of underestimating him," warned Blake. "He is one of the shrewdest criminal adventurers I have ever met in my whole career. He will bear watching —don't make any mistake about that. And now, shall we go along to the consulate? After that, we can complete matters."

A few minutes later they had entered a hired motor and were driving at reckless speed along the long, dusty road by the docks towards the town.

Why it is that, without exception, every native in the East insists on driving a car at a pace which verges every second on disaster no one has ever fathomed, but so it is; and neither threats, nor bribes, nor pleadings has the slightest effect.

As soon as the clutch goes in, one and all seem to be seized with a berserk madness, and the drive to the consulate they found was no exception.

After a score of wild, hairbreadth escapes they reached their destination, but with eyes and ears and mouths stiffed with dust and grit. As for the Chinese driver, no sooner had he brought the car to a stop than he relapsed into an attitude which suggested a tremendous weariness; but Blake and Tinker knew well enough that he would be galvanised into sudden life as soon as they started again.

To be quite honest, Tinker rather enjoyed the whole sensation, and offered to wager Blake that for every coolie's shirt-tail they flicked as they tore back they would not have a single casualty; but Blake was not encouraging any such nonsense, so Tinker was forced to bet with himself.

At the consulate they found that M. Pascal was personally known to the French Consul, and, as soon as he had assured Blake that everything was in order, they re-entered the car and started on the mad dash back to the docks.

Tinker's right pocket beat his left pocket in wagering, for they hadn't a single casualty, although there were two different occasions when it looked as if disaster must overtake them.

When they were on board again, Blake led the way to the purser's room, and that official took them along to the ship's strong-room. They waited outside while the purser got the smaller of the two packages which Blake had left in his safe keeping, then, after signing the purser's receipt, they returned to the smoking saloon.

As most of the passengers were ashore, they found the place deserted, so, seating themselves at a table in one corner, Blake broke the seal of the packet and undid the wrappings.

As he opened the small pill-box in which he had packed the pearls in soft cottonwool, and held out the two exquisite gems in the palm of his hand, the Frenchman gave a cry of delight.

There had been no exaggerating about the pearls of Benjemasin. His expert eyes saw that at the first glance.

They were pear-shaped, of identical size and colour, a soft rose pink, and, being matched so perfectly, would, he knew, bring an enormous price.

"They are lovely, lovely!" he exclaimed. "They are as good as sold to my native prince already."

"If you succeed in getting them through to him," said Blake jestingly.

But his words would not have been so lightly said if he had known that, while they sat enraptured over the gems, a man was lying in the shelter of a lifeboat on the deck just above the smoking saloon of the second-class quarters watching everything that was taking place through the window beneath which they sat.

Rymer had kept close watch on their every action, both before they had driven to the consulate and since they had returned. He had

9

felt pretty sure that the pearls had not been handed over to the stranger (whom, thanks to the telegram he had pieced together, he guessed was the agent referred to there) before they left the ship, for they had been in sight all the time, and he knew Blake was not likely to be carrying such a precious package, around with him.

Then, on their return, when they had disappeared below, he had guessed what their object was, and, when they had returned a few minutes later to enter the smoking saloon, he had hastily ensconced himself in a spot from which he could see practically all that was going on.

Rymer did not remain beneath the lifeboat long enough to risk discovery. His interest in Blake and Tinker was now finished. His mind was filled entirely with just one thought, and that was not to lose sight of the Frenchman.

So, as he had already sent his luggage ashore, he wriggled clear and made for the dock. He was seated in a hired motor outside the dock gates when Pascal finally appeared, and, as the Frenchman drove off, Rymer's car was close behind him.

Tinker went bodily through the window, and dropped on his knees in the room beyond. Like a flash he was on his feet, his automatic levelled. On a bamboo "charpoy" was a figure in white, alongside which stood two Celestials, shaken out of their Oriental calm by his sudden entry. *(Chapter 4.)*

AS soon as they had completed their business with M. Pascal, Blake and Tinker made arrangements to go ashore.

Tinker had already packed a couple of handbags, which would last them during the two days they would be at the hotel, so there was little to do.

Before leaving, however, Blake went along to the second-class quarters and made certain that Rymer had definitely left the ship.

A steward assured him that he, and all his luggage, had gone ashore, and, as the man did not mention that this had taken place only a short time before, Blake had no idea that Rymer had been on board at the time when he had handed over the pearls to M. Pascal.

They drove to Raffles Hotel, where they secured adjoining rooms, and, as it was then late in the afternoon, Blake left Tinker unpacking while he went down into the lounge to get a cocktail, and find out if there was anyone he knew staying at the hotel.

He succeeded in his first object, but not in his second, so, seating himself in a low cane chair in one corner of the palm court, he sat sipping his drink and smoking a cigarette while he idly watched the people about him.

He was seated thus when he caught sight of M. Pascal crossing the lounge. He signalled to him, and the Frenchman joined him. When he had ordered a sherbet, he said:

"Well; M. Blake, it is all fixed. I am taking to-night's train for Kuala Lumpur. By this time to-morrow night I shall have sold the pearls."

"And, I hope, profitably," said Blake. "By the way, what have you done with the rubies? You are not taking those with you, are you?"

"No. I have left them in the care of the Eastern Bank until my return."

"A good idea, I should say. Ah, do not turn too abruptly, monsieur, but presently look over your left shoulder!

"Three tables, from you, two men are seated. One —the one with the pointed beard —is the man of whom I told you on board, watch out for him. He would risk anything to get possession of those pearls, if he knew you had them. He is talking to a man whose features have a strong Chinese cast, although he passes as a European, I fancy he is part Chinese."

A few seconds later the Frenchman turned in a casual way and regarded the tables behind him. He noted the two men whom Blake had indicated; then he turned back.

"You are right, M. Blake. The one with the beard looks quite capable of being a nasty customer, as you British say. The other is, as you have guessed, part Chinese.

"I have seen him about Singapore quite a lot since I have been here. He has a very unsavoury reputation. I am given to understand that he is the owner of several disreputable opium and gaming places in the lower quarters of the town."

"I believe it," rejoined Blake." He certainly looks the part. And I'll wager if he and Huxton Rymer are together they can only be hatching mischief of some sort.

"I have an uneasy feeling, M. Pascal. Let me warn you to be on your guard. That man, Rymer, is as cunning as a fox, and as ruthless as a timber wolf."

The Frenchman tapped his pocket.

"I am prepared, M. Blake. They shall not trick me; and, besides, they do not know that I have the pearls."

"I wouldn't wager so much on that," remarked Blake slowly, "although, if they do, I can't imagine how they have discovered it."

"Still, news of that sort spreads like magic, monsieur. There are ten thousand Celestials here, in Singapore, who would gladly open your throat with a knife on the off-chance of securing such a prize as you are carrying with you."

They talked of other things until the Frenchman went off to pack. As Blake did not expect to see him again, he shook hands, and, although he had repeatedly warned the other to be on his guard, he did not dream for a single moment that that was the last time he was to see M. Pascal alive.

When next he was to lay eyes on him he was to find that his words had been too prophetic, for cold steel was to open up his throat, just as Blake had said.

Nor did Blake see the swift signal which went from the Chinese half-caste to a Chinese "boy" who stood with other servants at the back of the palm court.

Had he observed it, he might have seen this boy glide away on the heels of M. Pascal. From that second until death should claim him the watchful eyes of the East were to observe his every move.

He was doomed as irrevocably as if he had been sentenced by judge and jury without hope of reprieve.

Blake was not astray in opining that Rymer and the half-caste could only be hatching mischief.

Mischief it was, and a-plenty, for once he had trailed his quarry to the hotel, Rymer had lost no time in seeking out the man with whom he had conspired before, and whom he knew controlled the machinery which was just what he needed for his purpose.

It took them a very short time to come to terms, and then they had repaired to the hotel where Blake had seen them. Not that Rymer had suggested the killing of the Frenchman.

To do Rymer justice, he was no murderer, although there was little else he had not done, and would not do, in his lust for gain. He had killed, but it had always been in fair fight; and, although he knew perfectly well extreme measures might be taken by his half-caste associate, he stated firmly that this must not be.

John Ligan, whose origin was lost in the obscurity of that quarter of Singapore which hides so many of the deeds of darkness, has pledged his word that extreme measures would not be used, but without the faintest intention of restricting his agents to what he looked upon as squeamish sentiment.

He counted on pacifying his associate after the deed was done; and done it was, although of that Rymer was innocent. But of all the rest that followed he was guilty —guilty as sin itself.

Blake and Tinker were at dinner when M. Pascal once more passed through the lounge and emerged from the hotel. A Chinese boy carried his bag; and at his signal a car drew in at once before the steps.

The bag was handed in, then the Frenchman took his place. He told the man to drive to the railway-station; then he leant back, sniffing in enjoyment at the warm, scented night breeze which drifted lazily across from the gardens opposite the hotel.

His thoughts were of a pleasant nature, and it was not until they had left the well-lighted part behind them that he noticed the driver seemed to be taking a roundabout way to the station.

Nor did he know that, as they had driven away from the hotel, another car had started, and all the way had been keeping close behind them.

He bent over the back of the front seat and gesticulated and shouted to the driver.

The man apparently paid no heed, so Pascal resorted to curses and threatened violence. But the only result was to send the car at a more reckless pace than ever, and, as it lurched wildly, the Frenchman was sent back into his seat with a thud.

Along they tore at breakneck pace, getting deeper and deeper into the lower quarters of the town. Suddenly it dawned on the Frenchman that this was not the work of a pig-headed speed fiend, but for some reason he was being deliberately driven away from the station.

As the thought came to him a sudden fear clutched at his heart. He thought of the words of warning Sexton Blake had spoken. The next moment he had jerked out his automatic and was jamming the end of the barrel into the driver's back.

In response to the threat the fellow slowed down, and finally the car came to a stop.

It was only then that Pascal became aware that another car was pulling up close to him. He turned just in time to see half a dozen figures pile out of it and race towards him. He lifted his automatic and pulled the trigger again and again, but, to his chagrin, the hammer only clicked uselessly.

He knew then that someone had abstracted the cartridges from the clip. With a curse, he hurled the weapon into the face of the man in front; then he gave a loud shout for assistance.

The next instant the yellow horde came over the side of the car; the cry for succour was choked in his throat, he went down with a dozen hands clawing at him, a knife flashed, there came a queer coughing noise from the bottom of the car, then —silence.

BLAKE and Tinker had scarcely entered the lounge after dinner when Blake was approached by one of their fellow-passengers and asked to make one of a four at bridge.

Although he wasn't particularly keen on playing while ashore, he had been a consistent winner on the way down from Saigon, and could scarcely refuse.

Tinker went along and watched the play for a few hands; then, somewhat bored, he strolled back to the lounge, and, after idling about there for half an hour or so, decided to go for a stroll.

Singapore was no novelty to Tinker. He had been there several times before, and knew the place thoroughly from one end to the other.

In his work with Blake, it had been necessary for him to go into the worst quarters, and it was towards one of these districts he wended his steps after leaving the hotel.

Not that Tinker had any particular hankering to delve into the vicious life of the city. It was all an old story to him, and, truth to tell, he had been up against so many phases of it during the course of his work that he knew its sordidness for just what it was.

But, on the other hand, the staid and quiet never had appealed very strongly to Tinker, and with the inborn sense of adventure which was such a strong element in his nature, he turned naturally towards the part where, if at all, something might happen to break the monotony of the evening.

Even under ordinary circumstances it would have been injudicious for the lad to go poking about in the lower districts of Singapore, or, for the matter of that, in almost any foreign city one might care to name.

He and Blake were altogether too well-known —and unfavourably so —among the gentlemen of the underworld for either of them to take risks lightly.

But, unfortunately, that did not always enter into Tinker's mind. Had it done so on this occasion the evening would have had a very different ending for him.

There was a regimental band playing in the square opposite the hotel as Tinker emerged, so he strolled idly in its direction, puffing at his pipe and rather enjoying the distinctive odour of the East which hung like a heavy, invisible pall over the town.

The square was crowded with half a dozen Eastern races, with Malays and Chinese predominating, while there was a plentiful mixture of Eurasians, and not a few Europeans like himself.

The band was a good one, and was doing its best to the airs which had been popular at home a year before, but as Tinker had heard them all until he was weary of them, he soon forced his way through the crowds and made his way along towards the less staid quarter of the town.

He took his time, for he had the whole evening before him, and he knew that, once settled at the bridge-table, Blake would not be likely to rise for a good two hours or more.

Past the wider streets, where the more substantial business places are situated, he went until he came to the Chinese silk and curio shops.

He studied the wares as he walked, but found nothing sufficiently interesting to bring him to a pause until he was well into the quarter. Here the night life was very different from that he had left fifteen minutes before.

There was scarcely a sign of the West in the shops and houses, which were ablaze with lights, while the real business of the bazaar went on its way.

The crowds were so dense that even in the middle of the road it was difficult at times to force a way through. From every second house came the harsh blare of a cheap gramophone or a tinny piano.

Grog-shops were wide open, and more than once Tinker saw little groups of sailors making a riotous way along, intent upon seeing all the famous quarter had to show them before they returned to their ship.

It mattered not to them that before the night was over they would be penniless and wiser.

There were even a few pedestrians, who, like Tinker, stood out in sharp contrast to the others owing to the distinctive black dinner-jacket which they wore.

But in no case was one so garbed alone, with the exception of Tinker. Tinker didn't pay much attention to anything or anybody as he strode along. Now and then he caught sight of some den which brought up thoughts reminiscent of previous occasions when he and Blake had been there. But mostly his thoughts were on Huxton Rymer.

He and Blake had been discussing the adventurer at dinner, and both had agreed that the rapidity with which Rymer had got in touch with the notorious John Ligan was proof enough that it was Rymer's intention to pull off something in Singapore if possible.

Tinker had questioned Blake as to the possibility of Rymer trying once again to get possession of the Pearls of Benjemasin, but Blake had been inclined to think that these were now definitely out of his reach.

Naturally, that inference was the only one possible, for they knew nothing of what had happened to the torn telegram back in Saigon, and, of course, as far as they knew, M. Pascal was by then safely on his way to Kuala Lumpur.

Nevertheless, it was plain enough to both of them that a meeting between Rymer and John Ligan could have only one meaning, and Tinker was highly intrigued to know what they might be up to.

Along the unsavoury street in which he now found himself there were, he knew, a dozen or more dens belonging to Ligan, and he knew, further, that it was quite on the cards that at that very moment Rymer and Ligan might be in one of them laying their plans.

However, his speculations were purely idle, for, as he and Blake were due to leave inside forty-eight hours, Rymer's doings would not be likely to have any particular interest for them.

Almost unconsciously, Tinker turned into a much narrower and gloomier street than the one he had just been traversing, and it was not until he was some distance along that he realised that he had done so.

He drew up, intending to retrace his steps, but then, as he saw that it led to another well-lighted thoroughfare farther on, he continued his way.

He was just about half-way along, and was passing a small, shuttered house, which might have been anything from a gambling-den to a respectable Chinese merchant's abode, that he suddenly came to a pause and concentrated his gaze on the closed shutter nearest him.

It was no novelty to see a shuttered house in that part of Singapore, but it was out of the ordinary to come upon a closed window such as had attracted Tinker's attention.

It was a small house, flimsily-built, of a type so common in the native bazaars of the East. It was of wood, unpainted, and apparently of odds-and-ends of pieces picked up at random.

The ground floor consisted of apparently a single room in front, with, Tinker guessed, another at the back. There was a rickety balcony just above his head, on to which a couple of boarded windows opened.

On the ground floor just in front of him was a single-shuttered window and a blank door. It was this latter window which had brought him to a pause, for instead of being bare and unpainted like the rest of the house it was almost entirely covered by a weird-looking design painted on in a crazy mixture of yellow, vermillion, and periwinkle-blue paint.

Most of the design defied any effort to arrive at what it was meant to represent, but in the very centre Tinker could trace the outlines of a large "eye" such as the Chinese usually paint on the bows of their junks as a protection against the spirits of the water.

That was sufficient to tell Tinker that the place must be the abode of a Celestial, but it was because he had never seen the eye represented ashore that he was intrigued.

His first thought was that it was probably the house of a Chinaman who had formerly followed the sea, and who had brought his superstitions ashore with him, and it is ten to one that he would have passed on, mildly interested, had something not occurred at that moment to cause him to stand rigid, listening with every faculty.

It was a scream —a sharp, quickly-smothered scream, laden with some dreadful terror that had come, he was certain, from the room which gave off the rickety balcony just above his head.

Almost in the moment of its birth it had been choked into silence, but Tinker had heard enough to tell him that at that very second, close to him, someone was being tortured, that some Chinese fiends were pursuing their dark purposes upon some helpless victim.

Now, it is no unusual thing for the mystery and silence of an Eastern bazaar to be shattered by the scream of some tortured soul.

To interfere or make inquiries would be the very last thought of any of the other denizens of the place. It would be, too, the part of a wise man to walk on and ignore it, for only the very foolish or the very brave ever interfere in the mysterious doings which take place behind the closed shutters of the Celestial.

No one knew better than Tinker the folly of probing the meaning of that scream. He had had too much experience of the East not to realise to the full just how hazardous such interference was.

And yet, there had been something about that scream that had caused his jaw to set in anger. He would have wagered any odds that it had been emitted by some helpless woman. And because he was sure the victim was of that sex, it never occurred to him to worry as to what race she might belong.

Behind that painted window in that closed and shuttered house which bore such an extraordinary emblem on the blank shutter in front of him, some helpless being was being tortured in a way which has been brought to a fine art by the Chinese.

And because that was so —because he was either very foolish or very brave —you may decide for yourself —he was determined to find out just what was afoot.

He stood for a moment gauging the distance from the ground to the edge of the rickety balcony above. It wasn't far, for, like all the houses in the bazaar, the building was a small one.

He thought a good spring would carry him up. Quickly he brought out his automatic and slipped it in the side-pocket of his dinner-jacket.

Then he stiffened, crouched a little, and the next moment went up, his arms raised high, until his fingers grasped the wooden slats of the railing. It was a good leap, but no record-breaker.

With his hands gripping the slats, Tinker swung his legs in until his feet encountered one of the main uprights which supported the balcony.

Shinning up this, the while he kept moving his hands higher and higher, he managed in a few seconds to swing himself over the rail. He turned and looked into the street beneath.

As far as he could make out, the street was deserted, but that did not mean he had not been seen. He knew a score of pairs of eyes might have been watching his every movement from behind the innumerable blank shutters that hid so much teeming life of the night.

But he was not greatly concerned over that. What intrigued him more than anything was what mystery lay behind the shutters through which had come that scream of terror.

One stride was sufficient to carry him across the narrow balcony to one of the windows.

He trod lightly, and then stood listening. At first he could hear nothing, but after a few moments he caught the sound of a low, stifled moan.

That was enough for Tinker. Drawing back, he turned a little sideways, crouched as he was wont to do in a football-scrum, then he launched himself forward, striking the wooden shutter with the full force of his shoulder.

It would have taken a very much more substantial shutter than the flimsy one before him to withstand that impact. As it was, it gave way like so much rotten paper, and before he could check himself, Tinker went bodily through the window and crashed to his knees in the room beyond.

Like a flash he was on his feet, dragging out his automatic at the same moment. Then he stood on guard, bending slightly forward and peering at the strange sight which met his gaze.

The room was lit by a single flickering candle, which stood on an upturned packing-case at one side.

Close to this case was a low bamboo and coir-rope "charpoy," on which lay a figure clad in white. At first Tinker could not make out whether it was a man or a woman, but as he took a step forward he saw that it was a young Chinese girl clad in a white silk pyjama suit and strapped to the charpoy by thick coir-rope.

Standing close to the charpoy were two Celestials, for once shaken out of their Oriental calm by the dramatic entrance of the young European.

For at a single glance they knew that this clean-cut young man, so meticulously clad in his formal black dinner-suit, belonged to no roistering bands from one of the ships in port.

It was that startling discovery that held them unmoving long enough for Tinker to take note of the two wooden instruments of Chinese torture which had been attached to the girl's feet, and which had drawn from her that quickly-smothered scream of agony.

That again was enough for Tinker.

With a snarl of anger, he started forward; but in that same moment the two Celestials awoke to a realisation of what threatened them. With a squeal of rage one of them cleared the charpoy in a single leap and came for Tinker with a long knife held ready for action.

His companion followed, but before he could reach an effective position Tinker had jerked up his automatic, and as the shot crashed out the leading Chinaman fell back with a howl of pain, his knife-arm falling uselessly to his side.

Tinker plunged forward, shoulder down, and before the second Celestial could bring his knife into play he was sent crashing back against the wall. At the moment of his impact with that a surprising thing happened.

There came a splitting and a tearing sound of wood being rent asunder, and the next instant, to Tinker's amazement, the victim of his charge crashed clean through the flimsy partition and disappeared from view. There followed a further sound of crashing, a loud yell, then silence.

Without waiting to investigate the mystery, Tinker turned his attention back to his first assailant. It was well that he did so, for the Chinaman had recovered his fallen knife, and with it clutched in his undamaged hand, was in the very act of bringing it down upon the lad.

Tinker flattened to the floor like a wolf on the ice; then he came up again and drove his left full to the Celestial's jaw.

It was a beautiful punch, right to the point, and as if he had been hoisted bodily from his feet, the Chinaman went up, then back. He rolled to one side, and, like his companion, suddenly disappeared from view through the hole in the wall.

Tinker ran towards the place and saw at once what had happened. The thin wall had separated the room from a staircase leading to the floor below. The force of Tinker's charge had driven his antagonist clean through the wall, where he had rolled to the bottom of the stairs.

That explained the series of crashes which Tinker had heard — likewise the yell and the silence that had followed.

But Tinker knew there was no time to investigate further in that direction —if he was to get away. He hastened back to the bed, and as he bent over the instruments which held the Chinese girl's feet in their cruel embrace, his jaw set hard and his eyes glittered with rage.

"Yellow beasts!" he muttered, as he worked swiftly at the screws of the terrible device. "I've heard of these infernal contraptions, but I have never seen them in use before. Poor little thing! She looks as if she had fainted with the pain!"

But the girl hadn't, for as Tinker dragged the instruments clear and with a growl of anger hurled them through the opening in the wall, she opened her eyes and looked at him.

In them was no expression of gratitude or of any other emotion. They were as blankly non-committal as only the eyes of the Chinese can be. But Tinker made no attempt to question her.

He went on to the next part of his work, and when he had cut the coir-rope bonds which held her to the charpoy he stood up and motioned towards the window.

"You velly good! No use —I stay he'," she whispered in what Tinker recognised as Mission English. That meant she had received some education, at least, at one of the Mission-schools, and could understand him readily.

"You must come with me!" he snapped. "You can't stay here. No time to talk now, but I will get you to a place of safety. Come on! If we don't hurry up we'll have the whole bazaar after us.

"Here, take my arm and try! Take it easy until the blood gets back into your feet. That's the idea! Go easy —it hurts to walk, does it? Never mind; stick to it. As soon as the blood gets working in your feet you will be all right. That's it! Just a few more steps, and we will make it."

All the time Tinker was talking in encouraging tones he was assisting the girl across the room to the window. Not until she had stood up had he realised how very small and slight she was. He could easily have picked her up bodily, but he knew, if they were to make a run for it, her feet must get the circulation back into them.

The instruments had been clamped on her toes, and he had seen that the screws had been pressing the flesh hard into the bones. It had been a sort of an elaboration of the old thumb-screw torture of the Middle Ages.

He hadn't the faintest idea what had been the cause of it. Apart from the fact that he hadn't the time to ask then, he knew the girl might refuse to give him any information.

Still, he wasn't very much bothered over the reasons for it. The girl had been in an agony of pain and terror, and he had answered her cry. Singapore was a British port, despite the large Chinese population, and the British Raj said that this sort of thing must not go on.

It did go on, as everybody knew; and it always would go on while the Chinaman was what he was. At the same time, when an isolated case such as this did arise, then it was up to every decent European to stop it.

That was exactly what Tinker had taken it upon himself to do, and now, with his pulses hammering pleasantly under the adventure of it, he was determined to finish what he had started and get the girl to a place of safety.

He managed at last to get her to the balcony. It was his plan to lift her over the rail and drop her to the soft ground beneath; then to follow himself and make a run for it.

But just as he was about to lift her up the girl caught his arm and dragged him to one side as a knife whistled past within an inch of his ear and shot over the rail to be lost from view.

Tinker gave an exclamation and whirled, bringing his automatic up as he did so. He was just in time to catch sight of a figure coming towards him. He drove back into the room, firing as he went, and, as the weapon crashed, the Celestial, who, Tinker now saw, must have come from a room at the rear of the one in which he stood, turned and raced for cover.

He dashed through a door, which, until now, Tinker had not noticed.

Tinker was after him like a flash, kicking the door in even as the other slammed it in his face. As it gave beneath his weight, Tinker hurled it back, and then, on the very threshold, he drew up, utterly dumbfounded at what he saw.

Taking hold of the Chinese girl's wrists, Tinker unceremoniously lowered her over the balcony to the full length of his arms, and then let her drop. (*Chapter 5.*)

TINKER scarcely noticed that the fugitive Celestial had dashed through another door that evidently gave on to the staircase. His every faculty was concentrated on what he saw before him.

He could scarcely believe that it was not a grotesque trick of the flickering candle-light and his own imagination that were creating this stupefying thing which lay before him.

Slowly but steadily he moved forward, until he stood gazing down at the motionless figure which lay on a charpoy. The white face was like marble. The eyes were closed, and the jaw set in that rigid way that is only brought by one thing —death.

His eyes and his conscious sense told him that here, in this house in the heart of the Chinese bazaar, lay the Frenchman, M. Pascal, dead!

His reason told him that such a thing was impossible —that the Frenchman was by then well on his way to Kuala Lumpur. And yet — and yet, this thing before him was real enough. He reached out a tentative hand and touched the white mask.

Yes, it was real enough, he thought, as he drew his hand back. And yet what could it mean? What trick of Fate had brought him crashing through a shutter in that house of the painted window to find first, a young girl being tortured, and then, just as he was on the point of escaping, to come upon the body of this murdered European—for that he had been murdered Tinker hadn't the slightest doubt.

Tinker didn't pause then to try and figure out how the Frenchman had come to such a fate. He knew he must do just one thing —get back to Raffles' Hotel and inform Blake without any delay.

A crashing sound below assisted him in his decision. With a last look at Pascal he turned and dashed into the front-room and out to the balcony, where he found the girl still standing.

Without ceremony, Tinker picked her up, and, taking her wrists, held her over the rail. He lowered her to the full extent of his arms, then he let her drop to the ground.

Over the rail he himself went, and a second later landed easily beside her. Then he grabbed her hand, and turning, began to run towards the well-lighted bazaar street from which he had come.

That action was just as if he had kicked a hornets' nest to shreds, for with almost unbelievable rapidity, that quiet street was turned into a yelling pandemonium of human beings, who poured forth from doors and windows as if some gigantic eruption of Nature had spewed them out of nothingness.

There was no time now for either tactics or strategy —and there is a lot of difference between the two. It was a hundred yards or so to the immediate objective which Tinker had in mind.

Under ordinary conditions, he, being unhampered, could have sprinted it in ten seconds flat, but it was a very different thing to make it, burdened as he was with the Chinese girl, to whom every step was torture, and with a couple of hundred yellow devils trying to block his way.

His only hope was to drive a way through, and in attempting to do this he made free use of his clubbed automatic as well as of his feet.

He knew now that from behind the silent shutters of the houses many pairs of eyes had taken full cognisance of what had taken place at the house of the painted window.

Like so many land-crabs they had come pouring forth at scent of the quarry, and what was more, Tinker knew that he must kick them clear of him just as he would kick an army of land-crabs clear if he were to keep his feet.

Once he went down he would never get up again. That yellow swarm would engulf him, and there would be left just —nothing.

Once in the wider and better-lighted thoroughfare, he would be by no means out of the wood. But he knew he would stand a better chance there, for, although it would create a strange spectacle for a young European to go tearing through the bazaar dragging a Chinese girl along with him, there were plenty of Europeans about.

Even if they did not come to his assistance, they would be witnesses of what was going on, and in the fear of whom the Celestials would hesitate to take extreme measures.

Therefore he battered and kicked his way along, driving the mob to right and left as he went, seizing upon every opening to gain a few yards, bucking as if he were fighting his way down the football-field.

It was difficult to tell whether the girl were a willing captive or not. At least, she made no attempt to hold back, nor did she handicap his efforts to smash a way through.

With both hands free, Tinker would have been able to make better progress, but his left hand was fully occupied keeping a grasp of the girl.

After each advance he was driven back a little by sheer pressure of the yellow sea that was engulfing him, but he noted with satisfaction that, slowly but surely, he was gaining his objective.

Another twenty yards and he would be there. But just as that hope loomed up he caught sight of a Chinaman leaping towards him whose eyes were blazing with a murderous hatred that lifted his face completely out of the surrounding mob.

In some instinctive way Tinker knew that this fellow was connected in some way with the girl, and the next second, as she caught sight of him, she gave a sharp exclamation which confirmed it. There was murder, swift and sure, in those blazing eyes.

There would be no hustling of the European, trying to force him to the ground, where, under cover of the mob, he might be beaten to a pulp. This newcomer would strike in full view of whoever might be watching, and risk the consequences.

Tinker hadn't the faintest intention of being butchered by that yellow fiend if he could prevent it. But he knew, too, that here was no occasion for clubbing.

Only cold lead would stop the murderous devil, and even as the crazed Celestial drove the knife upwards towards his vitals, Tinker switched the automatic round and pulled the trigger.

The Chinaman went into the air and came down with a crash at Tinker's feet. Tinker pulled the trigger three times in rapid succession, shooting high.

The crowd gave back a little.

Tinker put one foot on the prostrate body of the man who had just tried to murder him and jumped forward, dragging the girl with him.

A lane opened ahead of him, and he broke into a run. He covered the remaining yards in safety; then, as he turned into the wider thoroughfare, the mob, temporarily held back by what had happened, broke into a renewed pandemonium of yells and tore after him.

Even the crowds of the bazaar, used as they were to strange sights, gazed wonderingly at the spectacle of the young European and the Chinese girl as they dashed along, pursued by the mob which swept into the street, and, as is always the case, automatically picked up reinforcements.

At that moment, just when it was most needed, there wasn't a European in sight. It seemed as if this must have spread like lightning to the knowledge of the mob, for their cries grew shriller, and Tinker knew his chances were very slim indeed of getting out.

He kept on plugging, however, and then, as he swung round a corner, he saw, just ahead of him, in front of a Chinese merchant's house, a motor-car. It was of a showy American type, such as the Chinese merchants of the Straits favour.

In the front seat was a Chinese driver, who was lounging at the wheel, apparently indifferent to the riot so close to him.

He came to life a moment later, however, as a young European climbed over the seat, and, taking him by the collar, threw him into the road. He had not been able to scramble to his feet before the car lurched, and for once in his life his Oriental calm was cracked as he saw the car go racing along at a mad pace, with the young European at the wheel and a Chinese girl clinging to the back of the tonneau.

Tinker gave that car all it had in it. They went along that street lurching from side to side in a way that kept them on the verge of disaster every second.

He didn't know exactly where it led, but he figured as it led away from the bazaar it must fetch up in some more desirable quarter.

It was a case of "any port in a storm," and any quarter in Singapore would have been more desirable to him just then.

The crowd had by no means given up the chase, for they could be heard in full cry behind.

Tinker didn't know whether the girl was still in the car or not.

As he had reached the car he had bundled her into the tonneau like a sack of flour, but he didn't know if she had jumped out afterwards.

He knew, at least, that, if she was still there, she would hardly attempt to get out while he was going at that pace.

Now, ahead of him, he could see another street, and began to slow down a little, intending to take the corner at a less reckless speed. But before he reached it something suddenly shot out into the road.

There was no time to avoid a collision, and, as he recognised it as a rickshaw, Tinker gave a yell and stepped on the accelerator again, he saw a terrified coolie go into the air and disappear.

There came a terrific crash as the car struck the rickshaw full on. There was a clatter and a scattering of broken wood as the car went through.

Then they skidded, struck a post at one side of the road, going through it like a match. Another lurch, and then, as Tinker got it straightened out and took the corner on two wheels, there came another roar and crash as the balcony which had depended on the post they had smashed came to the ground.

Tinker heard a new chorus of yells as he got the car somehow into the middle of the road, but he felt better paving beneath him, so he let it out full, and, as they roared along into the quieter quarter, the noise behind him died away.

Tinker did not slow down until he had left the bazaar far in the rear. As he drove along he saw that he was getting into the bungalow quarter, and a little later, when he swung into a quiet square, he recognised where he was.

It was the sight of a large, white building, set in a spacious compound, that gave him an idea. He drove towards it and drew up at the gate. Then he turned and saw the Chinese girl still clinging in terror to the back seat. Tinker grinned cheerfully.

"Nothing to be afraid of," he said. "You are all right now. Do you know what this place is?" And he indicated the white building.

The girl nodded.

"Him Canadian Mission," she answered.

"That's right; and that is where you are going," rejoined Tinker. "But first, I want a little information out of you. First your name, and why you were being tortured. Then I want to know what you can tell me about what I found in the back-room of that house.

"I want the truth, and I want you to tell me as quickly as possible, for I must leave you here and get away as soon as I can. Do you understand all I say?"

"Yes—undelstand. Me mission-gi'l at this mission."

"Ah! That is good. They will make no difficulty about taking you in. Now then, tell me what you can about that place."

With that Tinker consoled his jagged nerves with a cigarette, while the girl squatted on the floor of the tonneau and began to do his bidding.

Tinker put one foot on the body of the man who had just tried to murder him, and then jumped forward, dragging the girl with him. The mob, shrieking and yelling, broke into a pandemonium as the yellow fiends swarmed after him. (*Chapter 5.*)

"TELL me your name first," commanded Tinker.

"Sin-Len-Ye, honourable sir."

"And a jolly pretty one, too," muttered Tinker to himself. "Means 'Spring Blossoms' or 'Summer Blossoms,' if I remember rightly. Then aloud: "Why were you being tortured in that house?"

"Kwang-huen, my ga'dian, make sale of me to Tom Ligan — make sale as slave. I lefuse become plope'ty Tom Ligan. Him vel' evil man."

"Tom Ligan," said Tinker slowly. "Is he any relation to John Ligan?"

"John Ligan him fathe' Tom Ligan."

"H'm! So that's how it is, is it? Seems as if it is a case of like father like son! How much Tom Ligan pay?"

"Him pay to Kwang-huen five hundled dolla'."

"Whew! They must rate you high in the Chinese slave-market here! That is more than double the market-rate in Hong-Kong, So you refused to go, did you? Most Chinese girls would not dare refuse."

"I receif teaching at mission-school. I lea'n many things of the gleat West Countlee. I am the glandaugte' of Levelend Manchu. I no' go as slave to one half-caste, Tom Ligan."

"And I don't blame you," responded Tinker. "But that doesn't clear up matters. When I started out for a quiet stroll to-night I didn't dream that I would wind up by breaking into a house, stealing a Chinese girl, putting half a dozen Chinks out of commission, discover the dead body of a European, and wind up by making off with a motor-car. What to do now? That is the question."

"You have saf' me honoulable sir. I wish not make mo' wolly. I go now," said Sin-Len-Ye simply.

"No, you don't!" answered Tinker sharply. "If you think I am going to let you run loose at the mercy of that pack of yellow jackals you are mistaken. We will fix up something for you. In the meantime, you will have to stay here at the mission.

"They will take you in all right when they know what has happened, and particularly since you were once a pupil here. But first, I want to know what you can tell me about the dead man in the backroom of that house."

"I not know about him. To-night I make out noise in othe' loom, but I tied to bed and not see. I not know but Tom Ligan in that house,

32

and, maybe, John Ligan. I know no mo'."

Tinker nodded and turned back to the wheel.

"I'll wait until I tell the guv'nor what has happened," he muttered, as he steered the machine into the compound. "With the girl safe here at the mission, he can question her if he wants to."

The mission-house was in darkness, but after ringing for some time there was the sound of a window opening, and a voice asked in English what was wanted.

Tinker explained briefly, and evidently Sin-Len-Ye recognised the voice, for she called out and ran along the veranda. A few minutes later the door opened, and Tinker saw an elderly European woman holding a candle.

Briefly he introduced himself and explained sufficient of what had happened to account for his appearance there at that hour of the night with a young Chinese girl in his care.

The missionary had been more than twenty years in the East, and knew only too well how to read between the lines of what Tinker said. When he had finished she put her arm round the girl and drew her inside.

"Sin-Len-Ye will be safe with us," she said. "She was our pupil for some time, and is a good girl. I shall see that she is not a victim of this infamous bargain."

"I know she will be safe here, ma'am," said Tinker, "but the Ligan crowd are a bad lot from what I have heard."

"You have heard aright, young man. But I am not afraid of any of that yellow pack. The girl will be safe with us, and the Ligans won't dare touch her."

Tinker grinned as he returned to the car. "She's a game old girl!" he muttered. "She may be a missionary, but she is a fighter as well. I do believe she would give the Ligans a dose of buckshot if they showed up."

With his mind relieved of anxiety regarding the girl, Tinker could now give his whole thought to the sinister sight he had seen in the back-room of the house of the painted window.

There could not be the slightest doubt of the dead man's identity. Tinker was willing to take oath that it was Pascal, M. Acier's agent, who had received the Pearls of Benjemasin from Blake, and who should then have been on his way to Kuala Lumpur.

But what did it mean? What could it mean but one thing? If that dead man was Pascal, then it was a certainty that he had never reached the railway-station.

Between Raffles and that point he must have been waylaid and murdered. That being so, then someone must have known that he had gems of value on his person, and those unknown persons must now have the gems.

Both Tinker and Blake knew that Pascal was carrying the pearls. But who else could have known? Or did someone just suspect that he would have valuables on him —someone who had discovered that he was the buying-agent for a Paris gem-dealer?

Then there was the mention Sin-Len-Ye had made of the Ligans. It was certainly a strange coincidence that the house from which he had rescued a young Chinese girl who had been sold as a slave to Tom Ligan, the son of John Ligan, should also contain the body of the murdered Frenchman. Then suddenly Tinker gave a sharp exclamation:

"By heavens! Why didn't I think of that before? Tom Ligan — John Ligan, one of the worst half-castes in Singapore! That house of the painted window undoubtedly is one of the many owned by John Ligan.

"The Frenchman was taken to that house. John Ligan was hobnobbing at the hotel with Rymer. Back in Hong-Kong, Rymer did his best to get possession of the pearls. Is he behind this in a second attempt? It certainly looks darned fishy, and the sooner the guv'nor gets his thinking-cap at work the better.

"I have an idea he will be considerably interested in what I have to tell him. He takes a sort of personal pride in seeing that those pearls arrive safely in Paris."

Tinker's musings broke off as he turned into the square in front of the hotel. The band had finished its concert now, but the place was still brilliantly lighted, and there were still a good many people about.

Tinker did not think it advisable to drive the stolen car right up to the hotel-entrance, so he pulled into the side of the road by the garden. There he slid out, and was just turning to make his way the rest of the distance on foot when a fat, elderly Celestial appeared in front of him.

He gave every sign of having suddenly gone stark, raving mad, for he was waving his arms about and shrieking at the top of his lungs in half a dozen different dialects.

Tinker tried to dodge him, but the wild man kept blocking his way. Then Tinker understood.

"This must be the old codger who owns the car!" he muttered, grinning at the Chinaman. The grin was the cause of an even more violent spasm of shrill invective, but this time Tinker cut it short.

Lowering one shoulder, he drove forward, catching the Celestial full in his wide paunch. The shrieks broke off with a loud grunt as the fat man sat down suddenly in the road.

Without waiting for more, Tinker leaped over him and ran lightly round the corner to the hotel. A crowd was already beginning to gather, but before a Malay policeman could discover what was wrong, Tinker was inside the hotel and safe, for they wouldn't dare to follow him there.

He made at once for the small lounge, where he expected to find Blake still playing bridge. He was right, for Blake was sitting just where he had left him.

Tinker waited until the current hand was finished, then he signalled to Blake.

Blake knew every phase of the signals used by Tinker, and in this one he read urgency. He glanced at his score, then pushed his chair back, excusing himself.

"What is it, my lad?" he asked, as Tinker drew him aside.

"Can you break away from that game, guv'nor? I've had quite an experience tonight, and have a lot to tell you."

"Can't it wait?"

"No, sir." Then Tinker lowered his voice. "Pascal has been killed —murdered. And that means the Pearls of Benjemasin are gone again."

Blake did not betray by the slightest sign how amazed he was at the words. He merely nodded and said:

"Wait here. I will explain that I cannot continue."

With that he returned to the table, and after a few words of excuse and regret, rejoined Tinker.

"Come out to the main lounge," he said, taking out a cigar. "We can get a table apart there."

They found one isolated in one corner, and, after giving an order to the Chinese "boy," Blake leant back.

"Now, then, my lad," he said, "just what do you mean by your extraordinary statement?"

"Just what I say, guv'nor. Listen, and I will tell you everything that has happened since I left the hotel this evening. Oh, wait a minute, sir. There is that crazy old Chink whose car I borrowed without asking leave. I didn't think he would dare worry me in here, but I guess I made him about crazy when I butted him to the ground. I'll have to settle with him, I suppose."

"If I could only understand even a part of the statements you are making I might help you," said Blake irritably. "Do I understand that you helped yourself to the car belonging to that stout Chinaman who has just come in?"

"Guilty, my lord!" replied Tinker, with a grin. "I just had to. There were about five hundred yellow devils after my blood, and I had to make a run for it. The car was the only way. I banged it about a bit, but it is all right."

"I'll get the strength of this presently, I hope," said Blake testily. "Do you know who that Chinaman is?"

"Haven't an idea, guv'nor."

"It is Lee Sing, one of the best-known and most influential Chinese merchants in Singapore. I know him well, and like him. I am sorry you have offended him."

"Honestly, guv'nor, I couldn't help it. I had to have that car, and there was no time to ask permission. Then again, when he came on me like a lunatic, I didn't want to get mixed up in a mob.

"He was so fat I couldn't get past him, so I had to go over him. I am sorry if I have offended the old boy, and I am willing to apologise."

"From his point of view that would only make things worse, coming from a person of your age to one of his. You wait here. I will talk to him and soothe him."

With that Blake rose and walked leisurely across the lounge to where Lee Sing was standing, conversing in heated tones with one of the hotel-clerks.

Watching, Tinker saw Blake bow low, and saw the ceremonious response of the old Chinaman. Then Blake began to speak, and at a sign from him the clerk moved away.

For nearly a quarter of an hour they conversed, then Tinker saw them bow and part, Lee Sing turning to leave the hotel, while Blake returned to where Tinker sat.

"It is all right," he said, as he sat down. "I have made apologies and explained matters. I want to hear what happened in the bazaar.

"Lee Sing says the young man who took his car stole a young Chinese girl from a house in the bazaar. He is greatly excited over it, for he was about to approach her guardian to ask her in marriage for his son. Were you mixed up in that?"

"I should say I was, guv'nor. That is how the whole thing started. But if Lee Sing wants that girl for his son it is a good thing for him that I did steal her.

"She was going to a devilish fate —she had already been sold as a slave to Tom Ligan. She is safe now, and if I tell Lee Sing where she is perhaps he will forget about the car."

"You will be doing him a very great service if you can, and Lee Sing is not the man to forget. He seemed far more perturbed about the girl than about the car.

"But, so far, I am completely at sea, Tinker. I thought it might be possible for you to go out for one evening without setting the town by the ears.

"You seem, however, to have hit a good many of the high spots in the space of a couple of hours or so. Now then, begin at the beginning and tell me the whole thing.

"Exactly what do you mean by all this business of running off with a motor-car, stealing a Chinese girl, and then announcing that M. Pascal has been murdered and the Pearls of Benjemasin stolen?"

"Listen, guv'nor!"

With that Tinker bent forward and began talking in a low tone which did not carry past Blake. The latter had settled back to listen, but, as Tinker proceeded with his tale, Blake's attitude gradually stiffened, and by the time the story was ended, there was no doubt of the interest he felt in it.

In his eyes was that hard, steely look which Tinker knew so well, and which invariably presaged swift action on Blake's part.

Just a glimpse they were able to get of the figure bending over the steering wheel. But that glimpse was enough! Next instant Blake had bundled the Chinese driver out into the road. In one breath they uttered the name "Rymer!" (*Chapter 7.*)

BLAKE smoked thoughtfully for some minutes, then he said abruptly:

"There is no doubt that Pascal is dead?"

"None, guv'nor. I made no mistake on that score."

"Could you make out any wounds?"

"No, sir. You see, I had no time. It was nip and tuck as it was."

"You say this girl, Sin-Len-Ye, mentioned the Ligans?"

"Yes, guv'nor. As I have explained, she was sold to Tom Ligan, John Ligan's son, for five hundred dollars.

"She seems to think Tom Ligan was in the back-room when the body was brought there, and she suspects John Ligan of having been in the house."

"It was neither of the Ligans who was torturing her?"

"Well, I don't know Tom Ligan, but his father wasn't there. Besides, as far as I could see, the two men who were torturing her were full-blooded Chinamen, whereas the Ligans are half-caste."

Blake nodded.

"Tom Ligan looks more European than his father," he said. "But if what the girl says can be relied on, then it is a very significant thing that the Ligans were in the house to which Pascal's body was taken.

"It certainly begins to look to me as if Rymer knew in some way that I had handed the pearls over to Pascal, and that he sought Ligan's assistance in getting them.

"At the same time, I can hardly believe that Rymer would have a hand in coldblooded murder. He is a thief, and a criminal adventurer, but I have never known him to kill in that way.

"However, the arrangement may have been that, in return for a share of the spoils, Ligan was to get the work done, Rymer's contribution being the information he brought.

"At any rate, there seems to be a strong indication that the meeting between Rymer and Ligan here early this evening was to have some bearing on the fate that overtook Pascal after he left the hotel.

"I can't figure out how Rymer could have discovered that Pascal was to receive the pearls from me; but he must have done so. It may be that he already knew Pascal as a gem buyer, and seeing him with us, put two and two together.

"In that case, he may have been on board when the actual transfer took place. If we had only known that, we could have protected Pascal until he got away safely.

"However, the mischief has been done now. It seems that murder has been done, and I think it is a pretty safe conclusion to draw that the pearls have disappeared."

"What will you do, guv'nor? Will you advise M. Acier?"

"Yes. I shall file a cablegram to-night. Then we shall make a few inquiries. After that I shall decide what steps we shall take —if any. Our personal responsibility ended when Pascal received the pearls and gave me his receipt.

"But there are other factors to be considered, not the least of which is the connection we have already had with those same pearls which seem to be such a lure to Rymer.

"I want to have a talk with the young Chinese girl. After that we shall go to the bazaar and look into things there, though I haven't much hope that we shall discover anything important.

"Let us go upstairs and get into white clothes, my lad; we can't go digging about the bazaar at this hour of the night in dinner jackets."

Ten minutes later Blake and Tinker were once more in the lounge, this time clad in the white clothes of everyday wear.

They secured a car in front of the hotel, and when Blake had filed his cablegram to M. Acier, they climbed in.

Blake directed the driver to go first to the Canadian Mission bungalow, which, as when Tinker was there, they found in darkness.

But their repeated summons brought the lady missionary, and when Blake had introduced himself they were bidden to enter.

She conducted them to an airy sitting-room and left them there while she went to bring Sin-Len-Ye. The Chinese girl came in shyly a few minutes later and bowed low to Blake, as befitted a young Chinese person before an older and wiser individual.

Then she bowed to Tinker, smiling at him as she did so. Although Blake knew from Tinker that Sin-Len-Ye spoke English very well, he preferred to talk to her in her own tongue, for he knew that in this way he could follow more clearly the sometimes devious twistings of the Oriental mind.

As for Sin-Len-Ye, she showed instant gratification that the white man should address her in the tongue of her race.

"The young Honourable One has told me of what happened to-night," he said gently. "I want you to believe that I am here as your friend—that we are both your friends."

"Sin-Len-Ye listens and believes the words spoken by the Sacred One," she replied. "Were it not for the young Honourable One, Sin-Len-Ye would even now be at the mercy of the evil Ligan."

"Why did your guardian sell you to Ligan for a few hundred dollars when the wealthy and wise Lee Sing sought you in honourable marriage for his son?"

The girl flashed a surprised and shy glance at Blake. Then she lowered her eyes.

"If the Sacred One says that the reverend Lee Sing sought Sin-Len-Ye in marriage, then it is so. But Sin-Len-Ye knew not of this."

"Ah! Has Sin-Len-Ye seen the son of the honourable Lee Sing?"

"It is so, Sacred One."

"And you looked upon him with favour?"

"Sin-Len-Ye would have been greatly honoured to become the daughter of the wise and reverend Lee Sing, Sacred One."

"You did better work than you thought, my lad," said Blake swiftly, in English.

"It looks as if Tom Ligan had very nearly succeeded in breaking up a pretty little romance —a thing that is all too rare among the Chinese, where the girls of the family are valued at just the amount they will bring.

"There seems to have been a surreptitious affair between Sin-Len-Ye and the son of Lee Sing. The old merchant should he grateful to you for this."

Then Blake turned back to Sin-Len-Ye. "It is true that the wealthy and wise Lee Sing seeks you in marriage for his son," he said. "Lee Sing himself did tell me this to-night.

"To-morrow I shall inform Lee Sing that you are safe in the care of the good ladies of the mission, and he will come here to see you. And that will make you happy."

Sin-Len-Ye's little hands fluttered to her throat, and in her eyes it was easy to read that such a thing would be the greatest joy she could know.

At the same time, Tinker had saved her at the risk of his life, and according to her system of ethics she belonged to him as his property until he cared to release her.

Therefore she hesitated and glanced towards the lad, Blake

interpreted the glance and smiled.

"Sin-Len-Ye hesitates to reply, Tinker, because, according to her creed, she considers herself as your property. What do you say?"

"Great Scott! My property!" gasped Tinker. "I don't want her, guv'nor —I mean, she is a jolly nice little thing, but what on earth would I do, leading her around? Don't pin this on to me. Get me out of it someway."

Blake laughed.

"I don't think there will be any difficulty about that."

They had both spoken so fast that it had been impossible for Sin-Len-Ye to follow what was being said.

In any event, she would have to abide by the decision of this kind, honourable sir. But she hoped in her little fluttering heart that she might be allowed to go to the house of Lee Sing as his daughter.

She would not have been terrified if she had been claimed by this laughing-eyed young white man, who had carried her off just as the Manchu heroes of old carried off the fair princesses of the old realm.

All of which goes to show that little Sin-Len-Ye was not unlike many others of her sex, no matter what their colour. And Sexton Blake knew exactly what she was thinking. That was why he laughed again.

"I have spoken to the young honourable sir," he said. "He thinks that Sin-Len-Ye is a wonderful flower, but his duty makes it impossible for him to keep possession of Sin-Len-Ye.

"Therefore, sad as it makes him, he is going to be generous and release Sin-Len-Ye, so that she may become the daughter of the wise Lee Sing. But before he does so, he wants Sin-Len-Ye to answer as well as possible some questions that I am going to ask."

"It is the duty of the young to speak truthfully, Sacred One. It is the duty of the young to give respect to their elders. I listen."

"Who lives in the house where the young Honourable One found you to-night?"

"That I do not know, Sacred One. I have thought that it was an empty abode, but it is perhaps a house of the evil Ligan."

"When were you taken there?"

"It was during last night."

"You have told the young Honourable One that Tom Ligan was in the house tonight?"

"That is so, sacred sir. I heard him, but did not see him."

"And you think John Ligan may have been there as well?"

She nodded.

"You can tell me nothing about the dead man?"

"Nothing, sacred sir. He was brought to the house, I think, to-night. I did not know he was dead until the young honourable sir told me. But I knew something was taking place in the other room."

"Not much to go on here," remarked Blake to Tinker. Then he nodded towards Sin-Len-Ye.

"I shall not question you more at present, Sin-Len-Ye. But I may return tomorrow. To-night I expect to see the honourable Lee Sing. I shall tell him that you are safe."

Sin-Len-Ye rose and made a respectful obeisance first to Blake, then to Tinker. A gesture from Blake gave her permission to retire, and when she was gone Blake explained matters to the missionary lady.

Then he and the lad departed. As the car turned out of the mission compound, Blake said:

"She doesn't know anything about what connection the Ligans may have with the affair. I am convinced that she told us all she knew, and that she told the truth.

"We shall go on to that house now and see what we can see."

"By the way, guv'nor, do you remember me telling you that one of the shuttered windows was painted? What would that mean?"

"It may mean several things. I may be able to tell you when I see it. It depends on just what the design is, and also which window has been painted. My present guess is that it is a secret tong sign."

"If that bunch of Chinks recognise me again, we will have a warm time of it." remarked Tinker, as they turned into the main street of the bazaar.

"We won't have any trouble this time, my lad. You will find an entire lack of recognition, I fancy.

"The Ligan bunch know by now that the dead man in the back-room of that house has been discovered by a European, and they will watch from cover until they see what is going to happen.

"Just keep in mind that we are up against one of the most ruthless and influential gangs in the whole of the East.

"They have a thousand strings they can pull at any moment, and there isn't a single move in this sort of game they haven't played over and over.

"Just because we know that may give us a slight advantage, for if we go about the thing in an open and apparently a blundering manner, they may relax their guard.

"But what I should like to know more than anything else right now, is the whereabouts of Huxton Rymer. That gentleman is a mighty important card in this deal."

Blake said no more, for they had now reached the turning which led into the narrow street out of which Tinker had fought his way earlier in the evening.

To look at their surroundings now, one would never have guessed that such a riot had taken place.

The main bazaar was packed as usual, perfectly normal in every way. The side street was as gloomy and silent as when Tinker had first entered it.

It was difficult to believe that less than two hours previously a young European had dashed along that very street dragging a Chinese girl along with him while pursued by several hundreds of yelling Chinese.

Blake stopped the car just after they entered the street. Giving the Chinese driver instructions to wait, he led the way along until Tinker pointed to the small house where he had had his adventure. They stopped before it while Blake studied the outside. Then he gave his attention to the painted window.

"It is a secret tong sign, my lad. Just as I thought; but it is also an emblem of some superstitious belief.

"I fancy it has the effect of creating a sort of taboo of the house. However, everything seems silent enough. Let us investigate a little farther."

With that Blake mounted the step and began pounding boldly on the closed door.

Tinker stood close beside him, keeping an eye on the street. But not for a considerable time did any response come, and when it did, it was from the house next door.

An old Chinaman appeared, and, after bowing low, asked what the honourable sirs wished. Blake explained briefly that he desired to see the occupants of the house before which they stood.

"That will be impossible, honourable sir. The house has been unoccupied these many moons. Does the honourable sir see that which is painted on the window?

"That means, honourable one, that it would be unlucky to occupy the house, or even to enter it."

"An excellent scheme to keep people from nosing about the place," remarked Blake to Tinker. "However, I think we will risk the Evil Eye and break in."

He ignored the old man utterly, and together they jammed hard against the door. Under their joint pressure it crashed inwards, and they stood gazing into the dark interior.

Blake took out his pocket-torch and pressed the switch. Before them was a small room, along one side of which ran a rough counter, showing that the place had been used as a shop at some time or other.

But beyond that counter there was not another stick of furniture to be seen. Blake swept the circle of light from wall to wall and from floor to ceiling.

"Bare as Mother Hubbard's cupboard!" he remarked. "Step in, my lad, and close the door to keep that old liar outside. By now the whole street knows we are here and is watching."

Tinker pushed the door back in place, then he drew his automatic and followed the course of the pool of light which had been cast on the floor in front of them.

"Look at that, my lad!" said Blake, after a few moments. "Look closely at the floor and tell me what you see."

Tinker bent forward and studied the bare planks where the light fell. At last he shook his head.

"Can't see a thing, guv'nor, except dust."

"Dust. That is just it, Tinker. Dust is what I mean. If this house had been in recent occupation, then we ought not to find such a thick layer of dust as that on the floor."

"Well, it was occupied to-night, all right," protested Tinker. "I have made no mistake in the place."

"Um! Let us take a look at this counter."

Blake moved across to the rough board counter and held the electric-torch close. Then he touched the wood with his finger.

"Dust again, my lad. Thick, too. A little bit too thick, I am beginning to think. You say it was in the room above this that you found the girl?"

"Yes, sir."

"Well, there is a door leading to the back. Let us see what we shall find there. And keep that pistol handy, my lad."

Blake led the way to the door, which he kicked open. Then he stood aside while he flashed the light in and Tinker held his pistol ready.

But there was no need of such precautions. The room at the back was even smaller than that at the front, and was equally as bare, or rather, more so, for it had not even a counter.

Blake surveyed it in silence for some moments, then he stepped over the threshold.

"Just the same," he mused aloud. "Dust, dust, dust everywhere. Ah, a flight of stairs, Tinker! Up we go! I take it this is the flight down which you threw your two assailants?"

"This is the one all right."

"Curious," said Blake. "Here we have a staircase, which, according to you, must have been used quite a lot to-night. And yet every step is heavily coated in dust, my lad.

"Not a single print of any sort; nor was there one in the rooms below. Now, human beings can't move about in rooms as thickly coated with dust as these without leaving marks, my lad."

Tinker was puzzled, but he made no comment as Blake turned at the head of the narrow staircase and walked to a door on the right.

He pushed the door open, and once more they took precautionary measures. But here, as in the rooms beneath, they came upon nothing but dust and emptiness, with not a single stick of furniture or a print to be seen.

But off to the left of the hall Tinker pointed to what was obviously a hasty job at mending the thin wooden partition.

"There isn't any mistake about that job, guv'nor. It was through that hole I threw them."

Blake backed from the door of the room and studied the patched partition for some minutes. He made no comment, however, as he re-entered the room and began casting the light about.

"I take it this must be the room where you say you saw Pascal's body, Tinker."

"It is, guv'nor. It is empty now, and I don't understand it, but right over there against that wall was where the charpoy stood on which the body had been laid."

"Umm! All right. Now for the front room. This door, I take it, leads into it."

Blake opened the door, and still again they were greeted by the same scene of desolation. The room was utterly empty, and, like the other, had a thick coating of dust on the floor in which not a single print could be seen.

"This, I take it, is the room in which you have said the girl was being tortured, my lad."

"This is it, all right, and I'll soon prove it, guv'nor. The charpoys stood just there. That window is the one I burst in.

"If you will come across to it, I will show you. They may have mended it, but there must be some sign."

They walked across, and a few seconds' examination of the inside catch showed unmistakably that it had been hastily mended, and recently at that.

"Your story holds water, my lad," remarked Blake, as he turned back and surveyed the inside wall, which had been smashed when the Chinaman went through it under Tinker's rush. "Yes, decidedly so. And I will tell you what has been done.

"No sooner did you make your escape, Tinker, than they set to work to obliterate all signs of occupancy in order to have a complete reply to any charge that might be brought.

"They hadn't time to do a perfect job on the window catch and the smashed partition, but they counted on being able to produce any number of witnesses who would swear that both had been done a long time ago.

"They cleared out every stick in the place, and then began to lay a thick coating of dust. I fancy they began with this room, and, as they spread the dust, backed out in order that no prints should be left.

"Then the back room, and so on down the stairs to the lower floor. And I will say that they had done a good job —a deucedly good job!

"It is an old trick, and it usually works, but in this instance they overdid it to some extent. The layer is too thick."

"They must have moved, guv'nor! What do you think they have done with the body?"

Blake shrugged.

"Difficult to make a guess. It may have been incinerated, or it may be taken into the harbour during the night and sunk.

"One thing is certain —they will get rid of it to-night, if possible. With no body on which you base an accusation, and this deserted house to bolster up their denials, it is going to be a very difficult proposition to fasten it on to them."

"But they did it, guv'nor. Someone killed M. Pascal and got away with the pearls. Surely you are not going to allow it to rest there?"

"I didn't say that, my lad. But we won't get any 'forrarder' here. They have covered up their tracks too well.

"Certain things make us suspect that Rymer had a hand in this business, and other things seem to point to the Ligans, either one or both, of having been most actively mixed up in it. It is in that direction we must seek.

"But, first of all, we shall visit Lee Sing and have a short talk with him. In view of the fact that Sin-Len-Ye is safe, I have an idea he will be willing to do what he can to help us."

"If he forgets about the car," grunted Tinker.

"He won't hold that against you. Lee Sing is a very fine old gentleman, a true follower of Confucius and the Five Classics.

"We may as well proceed quite openly. The whole street will have its eye on us, anyway, and by now I imagine the bazaar will know also of our visit here."

Descending to the ground-floor, Blake led the way to the front. As he opened the door and emerged on to the street, not a single soul was to be seen.

Even the old Chinaman who had appeared on their arrival had taken himself under cover. Nevertheless both Blake and Tinker knew that a multitude of eyes was fixed on their every movement.

They gave no heed but walked leisurely along to where the car still waited. There was no question that the driver must have been highly curious to know why they had visited the house of the painted window.

Blake had a shrewd suspicion that he had been in silent communion with some of the residents of the street during their absence.

"Do you know the house of the wise and honourable Lee Sing?" asked Blake.

"It is known to me," answered the driver in a surly tone.

Blake did not speak again until he had stepped in. Then he bent forward, and the Celestial gave a terrified squeak as Blake's fingers ground into his neck.

"Answer my question civilly!" snarled Blake.

"Y-yes, wise and honourable sir! I know the house of the great and learned Lee Sing," stuttered the fellow.

"Then drive there —and see that you go carefully!" snapped Blake, as he released him.

Whatever the driver's thoughts may have been, he suppressed them, for he had no hankering to test the white man's threat.

Therefore, he turned the car carefully and drove slowly through the crowded bazaar until he came to the street from which Tinker had so unceremoniously taken Lee Sing's car earlier in the evening.

They had just turned into the street when, in the bazaar behind them, a loud pandemonium broke out. Loud yells split the air.

Blake motioned for the driver to pull into the side of the road while he and Tinker looked back to see what was the cause of the uproar.

The yells grew louder and louder as the sound of the siren approached; then they saw a wild scattering of the crowds at the end of the street, and the next second a powerful car tore past and disappeared.

Just a fleeting glimpse they were able to get of the figure bending over the wheel driving as if seven devils were after him. But that glimpse was enough for both Blake and Tinker. In one breath they uttered the name:

"Rymer!"

The next instant Blake was over the back of the front seat, and, without ceremony, lifted the Chinese driver into the road. Tinker followed him, and was jerked down with a thud as Blake threw in the clutch and manoeuvred to turn. He made it at the risk of capsizing.

Then he sent the car forward, while Tinker leant over and started the hooter going. They swept into the main bazaar street, sending the yelling crowds to right and left as they fled to escape this new menace.

Then Blake let her out, and while Rymer's car had now disappeared from view, the cloud of dust he had raised left a trail that a blind man could have followed by sheer sense of smell.

John Ligan went back, clawing and cursing, a bullet through his shoulder and another through his left lung. Tom Ligan had fired twice, but missed, and was now diving for cover. (*Chapter 8*.)

The Eighth Chapter.   Double Crossed.

IF Sexton Blake had guessed for a single minute that events regarding the Pearls of Benjemasin were to move so swiftly, he would have pursued very different tactics.

He realised this before that night was over. On the other hand, Blake can hardly be called short-sighted because he went first to the mission and then on to the house of the painted window before making an attempt to locate Rymer.

It must be remembered that, in the first place, Blake was no longer responsible for the pearls. Secondly, he had made up his mind that he would not interfere with Rymer, providing the other obeyed his injunction to leave the Amiral Lebon at Singapore.

M. Pascal was an experienced man, who had been one of M. Acier's principal and most trusted gem buyers for many years.

He had been warned by Blake that an attempt had been made in Hong-Kong to get possession of the pearls, and at the hotel in Singapore, Blake had even pointed out Rymer as the adventurer chiefly interested in them.

That should have been sufficient for a man of M. Pascal's experience, and regrettable though his fate was, it cannot be denied that he might have avoided that tragic end if he had taken Blake's warning more to heart. Over-confidence in himself had been his undoing.

Furthermore, not until Tinker returned after his exciting experience at the house of the painted window did Blake know anything of what had been going on during the evening.

Following that, he only had what Tinker was able to tell him on which to base a theory as to where the pearls might now be.

There was the conversation between Rymer and John Ligan, a known crook, in the lounge of the hotel early in the evening. There was his own knowledge that Rymer would make another attempt to gain possession of the wonderful pearls if he thought for a single moment that he stood a sporting chance.

But here it must be remembered that up to then Blake was under the impression that Rymer thought the pearls still in his possession, and, hence, locked up safely in the strong-room of the Amiral Lebon.

Blake knew nothing of the fate of the torn telegram back in Saigon; nor did he know how Rymer had lain concealed under the lifeboat on the deck above the second-class smoking saloon watching the actual transfer of the pearls from Blake to Pascal,

But Blake trusted Tinker's word implicitly. If the lad said he had seen the dead body of Pascal lying in the back room of the house of the painted window, he had seen it.

There could be no mistake about that. Tinker had been too well trained under Blake's guidance to commit himself to such a statement unless he was positive whereof he spoke.

In Blake's profession there was no room for mistakes of that sort. Ergo, Pascal was dead; Pascal had carried with him the Pearls of Benjemasin. Rymer must in some way have discovered that fact; Rymer had been in confab with a half-caste who was one of the deepest and worst crooks in the East. It wasn't a very wild theory to jump to the conclusion that the chain would lead from that meeting to the death of Pascal.

That was Blake's private opinion. But there was no reason why he should assume a personal activity in the affair.

All that he was called upon to do was to report the matter to the police, have Tinker make a sworn statement of what he had seen, cable M. Acier what had happened, and make an additional report to the French Consul.

With that his duty would be done. But Sexton Blake did not always confine himself to just the act of duty.

In a case like this one there were personal considerations which influenced him to probe matters more deeply, and it was for that reason he had determined to go to the house of the painted window before making any very active efforts to locate Rymer.

Just because Rymer had been seen talking to John Ligan —just because Ligan was known to be a "bad 'un," was not sufficient for Blake to suggest their detention by the police.

He would need to have more direct evidence than he had before even the French Consul would feel justified in taking things up with the British authorities.

And it was at the house of the painted window that he had hoped to come upon something which might give him a clue to that further evidence.

He had not been unaware that a clean sweep might have been made, just as he and Tinker found to be the case.

He had, in a way, anticipated that, for he knew the ways of crooks well enough to realise that Tinker's visit there would create consternation, even though his identity was not known.

On leaving the house of the painted window he had considered the next best move would be to have a talk with Lee Sing and tell him just what had happened.

Lee Sing's position in Singapore was not unlike that of the wealthy Lee Won in Hong-Kong, to whom Rymer had tried to sell the pearls, and who had been of no little assistance to Blake when the latter had planned their recovery.

Like Lee Won, Lee Sing was of the Four Lakes Tong, one of the most powerful secret societies in China, a society which was one of the few which really had the regeneration of China at heart.

It is well-known that Sexton Blake had been of no little service to the Four Lakes Tong in the past.

It was also well-known to the Four Lakes Tong that Sexton Blake had been the most powerful factor of opposition to Prince Wu Ling, of the Brotherhood of the Yellow Beetle, a brotherhood that had been threatening for some years to engulf the Four Lakes Tong.

For these reasons every councillor of the Four Lakes Tong felt more than friendly towards Blake, and was keenly anxious to do what he could at all times to repay the debt which the tong owed to Blake.

There is an extraordinary depth of gratitude among the Chinese of the better type.

Therefore, while it was unfortunate that, in his desperate need, Tinker had been forced to make off with Lee Sing's car, and, farther, in trying to avoid the irate merchant, he had butted him in the paunch, which, among the Chinese, is known as the Seat of Wisdom, and, therefore, to be respected accordingly, the contretemps had, after all, been fortunate, for, on his part, Tinker had something to offer which was very much desired by the son of Lee Sing.

This is, generally speaking, the line Blake's thoughts took after Tinker had made his report at the hotel.

And if it had not been for the sudden appearance of Rymer, driving a car at a pace that told its own story, it is safe to say that Blake would have carried out his intention of visiting Lee Sing.

But no man would drive a car through that crowded bazaar unless he had some very urgent reason for doing so, and when that man was none other than the notorious adventurer, Huxton Rymer, it is not to be wondered at that Blake immediately construed that it was more than likely Rymer's desperate speed had some connection with the events of the early evening.

Nor was he mistaken, for Rymer had more cause than Blake thought to get out of that bazaar as fast as the mechanical contrivance he was driving would take him.

Had Blake been present at an interview which was taking place even as he and Tinker were examining the interior of the house of the painted window, he would have understood better.

Blake had made no mistake in thinking that Rymer and John Ligan had been discussing ways and means to get possession of the Pearls of Benjemasin.

It is already known that almost immediately on landing in Singapore Rymer had sought out the half-caste crook, and had passed on the information in his possession.

Through Ligan's agents it had been an easy matter to find out from Pascal's Chinese room-boy that the Frenchman was on the point of taking his departure, and when he had emerged from the hotel he hadn't a chance of taking any other car than the one which had been "planted" ready for him.

Up to this much Rymer was a willing accomplice. Personally, he didn't care two pins what John Ligan might do in his private affairs. They were no concern of Rymer's.

He knew a good deal about the various dens in Singapore which Ligan owned and operated, and he knew, too, that there was many a dark deed done in those dens which never came to light.

That was Ligan's look-out. In this business they were temporary partners only, and it was in this only that Rymer was interested in keeping Ligan within bounds.

From his point of view it was entirely unnecessary to resort to extreme measures to get the pearls away from Pascal.

As a matter of fact, Rymer was right in that, and the extreme measures taken by Ligan were a great mistake from a tactical point of view, aside from the criminal phase of it.

Even in Singapore it is no easy job to make away with a European without very pressing inquiries resulting. That was what Rymer realised. But Ligan had gone unscathed for so long he felt himself invulnerable in the deeps of the bazaar.

He was such a powerful factor that he took it upon himself deliberately to refrain from instructing his men not to kill the victim. That was why as soon as Pascal made a fight of it his fate was sealed.

After their conference at the hotel, Rymer and Ligan had gone to the native quarter, and, in an upstairs room of the house which Ligan usually favoured as his bazaar headquarters, Rymer had waited while Ligan made the necessary arrangements.

It is known how unerringly they were carried out. During this time Rymer and Ligan had been sitting talking while waiting for reports of the result.

Rymer had regaled Ligan with an account of what had happened in Hong-Kong, and how, at Saigon, his quickness in salvaging the torn pieces of Blake's telegram had put him on the track of the pearls.

"Considering what expense and trouble I have already been to on account of those pearls, it would be only fair if my share was two-thirds, and yours one-third.

"All you have to do is to give instructions based on my information. But I am no hog, and in the settling-up I am quite agreeable that we should split fifty-fifty, or I will pay you a fair cash price for your pearl."

"Unless I make you a cash offer for yours," interpolated Ligan.

Rymer nodded.

"Why, that suits me, too," he rejoined. "Any fair way for a split is agreeable to me."

It was just then that Tom Ligan, John Ligan's son, entered the room.

Like Rymer and his father, Tom Ligan was dressed in a silk suit of European cut. His features were more the European type than those of his father's, although he had the oblique eyes and flat cheek-bones of the Chinaman.

Like all Eurasians, he had a profound contempt for the Asiatic race whose blood ran in his own veins, forgetting that in the crossing only the worst qualities of that blood had been given him.

John Ligan was about as bad as could be imagined, but he had a worthy successor in his son Tom, who had absorbed every single known trick of evil, and was in a fair way to invent some new ones on his own account.

Even Rymer made up his mind as he studied him that he would not trust him quite as much as he would an enraged cobra.

It was evident that Ligan the elder was perfectly acquainted with his son's doings, for no sooner had he entered the room than Tom Ligan said:

"I want you to take a hand for me. There is the devil to pay."

"What is the trouble, Tom?" asked the father.

"It's about that crazy old fool, Sin-Len-Ye's, guardian. Sin-Len-Ye is fighting against the sale, and the old man won't close the deal until she actually arrives at my house."

"Where is she now?"

"At the house of the painted window. I dared not bring her any further. She was kicking up an awful rows and Lee Sing's place is too near there for me to take the risk.

"Her guardian says he is afraid of Lee Sing, and won't budge until he sees the girl inside my house. What to do!"

"That's mission education for you!" snarled John Ligan. "I always said it was a mistake. If she had been kept in her place, as she ought to have been, she would have accepted her fate and been thankful for it!"

"It isn't that so much as Lee Sing's son. As far as I can find out, they saw each other at the mission-school, and they think they are in love!" Tom Ligan sneered.

"But it has got to be settled, do you hear? I don't want Lee Sing raising a riot there to-night. I have other business afoot."

"Well, so have we!" growled his father. "We are waiting now to hear about a certain matter. As soon as I know how things have turned out I will come along with you and see what I can do."

"I know what you are waiting for," put in Tom Ligan. "You can hear just as well if you come along to the other place with me. The job has been finished, and you will probably meet Kai-Wo on the way."

"How do you know this?" asked John Ligan quickly.

The son grinned.

"Never mind! I know it all right! Besides, there is something else you ought to see at the house of the painted window."

For a moment the eyes of father and son met.

Rymer, who had been listening idly, pricked up his ears at Tom Ligan's last words. He was not pleased that the son should know so much about the business on which he and John Ligan were engaged, and he knew that pair of crooks well enough to suspect that some message had passed between them in that swift glance of understanding.

Immediately after that John Ligan rose. "All right!" he growled.

"I will come along with you; only I can't see why you don't handle your own affairs. You stay here, Rymer, until I come back, I shall not be long. Tom says the job has been completed, so we can settle up as soon as I get back."

Rymer was not satisfied with this, but he could hardly make an objection just because he was suspicious, so he nodded an assent.

"Don't be long," he urged. "You know my present position. I want to complete matters and make arrangements for getting away."

"I'll be back inside half an hour."

With that the two Ligans took themselves off while Rymer filled his pipe and sat smoking impatiently.

Tom Ligan had been quite right when he had said that the job had been completed.

Pascal had already been murdered, and his body brought to the house of the painted window. But Tom Ligan knew all about that business from his father, even though the elder had made a show of being surprised at his words.

Tom Ligan had known, too, that Pascal's real fate was not to be told to Rymer, for the two had already determined between themselves that not only was Rymer not to be permitted to get out of the bazaar with his share of the spoils, but in case of inconvenient inquiry, the murder of Pascal was to be fastened upon Rymer.

Which goes a little way to show just what a priceless pair of ruffians they were.

But, unfortunately for their plans, Kai-Wo, Ligan's agent, who had had charge of the attack on Pascal, did not come to Ligan's house by a direct route. It is just little accidents like these that oft-times alter the whole course of events.

Kai-Wo had several stains on the sleeve of his jacket which he had received during the struggle, and as Kai-Wo was a very deep old villain he was anxious to get those stains removed as soon as possible.

So, after seeing the body of the murdered man safely delivered in the backroom of the house of the painted window, he had started out to take the news, plus the loot, to John Ligan.

But he had gone first down a side-street to his own modest abode, where he had changed his jacket for a clean one, and had given orders to his withered spouse to get the other one washed before his return —or he would try a little private torture on her.

Then he had made for Ligan's house. But the two Ligans were

already on their way in rickshaws to the house of the painted window, and thus it was when Kai-Wo arrived at Ligan's headquarters and entered the room where he expected to find John Ligan, he found only Huxton Rymer.

Now, Kai-Wo was one of John Ligan's most trusted henchmen, and as much in Ligan's confidence as any of the numerous agents he employed.

More than that, Kai-Wo was just as deep and cunning a Celestial as could be found in the East, and before he tackled that job on the night in question he had known as much about matters as Ligan himself.

He knew, for instance, that Rymer was a partner in the affair, and that it was Rymer's information that had made it possible.

He had seen Rymer with Ligan before, and therefore classed him with Ligan. But what he did not happen to know was that Rymer was not to be allowed to know that Pascal had been murdered.

The Ligans had not yet confided to Kai-Wo their secret plans for Rymer's undoing. And while Kai-Wo would not hand over the pearls to anyone but John Ligan, he saw no reason for not regaling Rymer with a full account of what had occurred.

Thus it was that while John Ligan and Tom Ligan stood in the upstairs backroom of the house of the painted window, while preparations were being made to apply the torture to little Sin-Len-Ye, in order to make her listen to reason, and while Tinker was starting out from the hotel for his evening's stroll, Rymer was learning that the very thing he had qualified should not be done had been carried out.

Rymer was too wise to show any signs of surprise at the revelation. On the contrary, he nodded as if pleased, and went so far as to commend Kai-Wo on the manner in which he had carried out his work.

But as soon as he could he got rid of the Chinaman, sending him downstairs to wait for Ligan's return.

Rymer wanted to think, and he knew he had a very short time in which to do so. He knew now the peril of his position. He knew the Ligans too well not to be able to grasp now the meaning of that look which had passed between them.

Tom Ligan had known that Pascal had been murdered. He had come from the house of the painted window where the body lay. He had given this message to his father by that glance, and the two had gone off.

"Curse them —curse them —curse them!" whispered Rymer sibilantly. "I didn't think Ligan would try to double-cross me on such an open-and-shut case as this. I ought to have tried to pull it off alone.

"What a fool he has been to have the man killed. And with Sexton Blake right here in Singapore it was madness. But it isn't Ligan who will see a noose dangling over his head if he can help himself. Someone else always has paid his debts of that nature, and someone else will pay this debt if he has his way.

"And the person who will pay it is I —I, Huxton Rymer. Let me think —let me think! I must outwit that yellow mongrel some way."

Rymer was to have plenty of time for thought. Had he wished he might have made his "get-away" without hindrance, but he was determined not to go until he had seen the Ligans, had a show-down, and got possession of his share of the loot.

Huxton Rymer was no apprentice. In his way he was just as cunning and hard-bitten as John Ligan, only there was this essential difference between the two men.

One worked entirely from the angle assumed by a man of full European blood, from the ineradicable prejudices against some things that no amount of criminal adventure could drive out of his nature— the other took as naturally to the dark and devious as a duck to water.

After nearly an hour had passed Rymer went downstairs to see if Kai-Wo was still in the house. He could not find him, but even if he had done so he would not have tried to take the pearls from the Chinaman by force, for he knew a single cry would bring a hundred yellow jackals upon him, and his chances of getting away would be nil.

He idled in the big public-room on the ground floor for some time watching the games of fan-tan in progress; then he returned to the room above.

Another three-quarters of an hour went by, and in growing impatience Rymer rose once more to make investigations. He was beginning to feel very uneasy.

By all reckoning John Ligan should have returned an hour and a half ago. His long delay made Rymer suspect that the noose might even then be in preparation, so that when it fell it would fall on his neck.

He moved cautiously out of the room and went along a dark passage towards the back of the house. He knew the quarters there were private to the use of John Ligan, and he knew, too, that there was a staircase at the rear, and he wanted to refresh his memory as to the lay-out of the place.

He had reached the top of the staircase, and was gazing down into the black pit beneath him, when suddenly he heard the sound of a door opening. At the same instant he caught sight of a line of yellow light, and as he drew back, peering over the banisters, he saw some figures stagger through the doorway, carrying some sort of a heavy load.

Rymer crouched low until he made sure that the party intended coming up the stairs. He drew back inch by inch until the flickering light of a candle lit up the features of John Ligan, who was following at the rear.

Then Rymer turned and sped back to the room where he had been waiting. He knew now what that burden was, but what puzzled him was why it had been brought from the house of the painted window, where, according to what he knew of that house, it should have been safer than any other place.

He was sitting back smoking when John Ligan finally appeared, but close at hand, in the outer pocket of Rymer's silk coat, was his automatic. He nodded surlily to Ligan as the latter walked round the table and dropped into a chair.

"You have been away a nice long half-hour," growled Rymer. "Kai-Wo showed up just after you left and said everything was all right. Have you seen him?"

"Yes. I couldn't get back sooner, Rymer. There has been the very devil to pay. Kai-Wo exceeded his instructions, and they finished off the Frenchman. They took him to the house of the painted window. He was there when I got there.

"As the damage was done there was nothing for it but to make plans to cover it up. I fixed up Tom's trouble all right and gave instructions what to do with the Frenchman. I was on my way back here when I was overtaken by an urgent message. I had to hurry back."

"What happened?"

"Nothing worse could have happened. Just after I left, it seems that a young fellow —European —who was strolling through the bazaar happened to pass the house of the painted window.

"He must have heard what was going on in the upstairs, for he climbed the balcony posts, kicked in the shutter, and, after kicking the two men there through the wall and down the stairs, released Sin-Len-Ye and put her over the balcony.

"Kai-Wo, who had arrived just then, gave the signal, and the whole street turned out. The others in the main bazaar tried to block him, too, but somehow he managed to get away, and took Sin-Len-Ye with him."

"Well, how does that affect us? What have Tom Ligan's affairs to do with us? We plan a certain job, and it is carried out. You first allow your men to complicate things by killing the Frenchman. That was a fatal mistake.

"I knew what I was talking about when I told you it mustn't be done. Yet you allowed them to do it. On top of that, you permit Tom Ligan to bring his personal schemes into this.

"That is no way to work, and you know it! This job should have been carried out as I stated. And we should have had a settlement two hours ago. Now, what about it?"

"Wait a minute. You don't know the worst yet. While that young European was in the upstairs room Kai-Wo was foolish enough to go after him. The fellow got the better of Kai-Wo, and as Kai-Wo tried to gain the back-room the fellow followed him and saw the body of the Frenchman on the bed."

"My heavens! And after that he got away?"

"Yes."

"And you call yourself clever!" sneered Rymer. He broke off just then as Tom Ligan came into the room. "What do you want now?" asked Rymer truculently. "Haven't you mixed up enough for one night in our affairs?"

"Not quite," responded the other. "I heard you demanding a settlement. That is why I am here. What settlement are you talking about? We haven't anything that belongs to you. What are you doing here, anyway?

"They say a Frenchman has been murdered to-night, and there are rumours in the bazaar already that it was a bearded European who did it. That seems to answer to your description, and as we don't want to be mixed up in anything of that sort, you had better clear out. Isn't that right, father?"

Rymer had listened grimly to the full revelation of the astounding double-cross the Ligans were trying to hand him. It was exactly as his instinct had told him.

And through that instinct he had been prepared for just such a show-down. He knew that Tom Ligan had probably been standing outside the room listening to all that was said, waiting to make his appearance at what he considered the right moment. But scarcely were the last words out of his mouth than Rymer had kicked his chair back and was on his feet, his automatic sweeping from one to the other.

"A lovely pair of crooks you are!" he said softly. "A very clever pair, but I have had your number ever since Kai-Wo came here. You didn't know that Kai-Wo had told me the Frenchman was murdered. You didn't guess that I suspected that when your whelp came in the room the first time.

"I knew as soon as you had gone why he wanted you at the house of the painted window. And I know, too, you crooked yellow mongrels, that the body was brought back here just now. I was at the head of the stairs when you came.

"I have been waiting just until the show-down came, and now I've got you. And by the great toe of the Buddha, you will pay up! Our agreement was a fifty-fifty split.

"I am not very particular, and in double-crossing me I owe you nothing. But those were the terms, and you will live up to them. Now, whichever one of you has the loot roll one of the pearls across the table. Then I'll go, and not before.

"Begin before I reach ten, for then I am going to do some fancy shooting. Now—"

Not the vestige of an expression had shown on the face of either son or father while Rymer talked, but now, as he finished, Tom Ligan threw himself to one side, clawing for his pistol as he lurched. In the same instant John Ligan lifted the table bodily and sent it hurtling towards Rymer. But Rymer had been on guard, and twice his pistol crashed out.

John Ligan went back, clawing and cursing, a bullet through his shoulder and another through his left lung.

Crimson flecked his lips, but he was still conscious, and he struggled with what little remaining strength he had to reach his weapon and "get" Rymer before his senses fled.

Tom Ligan had fired twice, but his aim had been bad, owing to the fact that he was still moving for cover.

Rymer dived behind the upturned table, then threw himself to one side, and the two weapons crashed at the same moment.

A piece of wood flew against Rymer's cheek as the bullet from Tom Ligan's pistol ripped through the table. But Tom Ligan would never pull another trigger, for Rymer's bullet hit him fair between the eyes.

As he fell back, Rymer sprang to his feet and made for John Ligan. Forcing the wounded man back, he began swiftly going through his pockets until he came upon what he sought —one of the pearls.

But only one did John Ligan have.

Rymer knew instinctively that the division of the spoils must already have been made between father and son, and he was just on the point of crossing to the huddled figure that had been Tom Ligan when there came a whistling sound close to his ear and a knife stuck quivering in the wall close to him.

Rymer ducked and whirled, shooting fast as he did so. He was just in time to fall to one side as a second knife flew towards his heart, and then Kai-Wo, who had been standing just inside the door, crashed to the floor. Rymer waited for no more.

He knew that the sound of the shooting would bring a mob from the lower floor. He was tempted to wait and search Tom Ligan for the second pearl, but he knew the risk was too great. He sprang across the room and raced for the back. He dashed down the rear staircase and fumbled about until he found the handle.

Then he jerked the door open and sprang out into the narrow lane at the back. He ran along that until he came to a wider street, and turning again to the left, reached the main street of the bazaar.

Two or three motor-cars were to be seen, and with the same audacity Tinker had employed not long before, Rymer commandeered the first one he came to.

He jerked the Chinese driver bodily into the road and took his place. Then he started off, reckless of whom he might strike. He knew his only hope of escaping the Ligan pack was to cut his way out of the bazaar before they could engulf him.

And thus it was that, tearing along as if the seven fiends were after him, he was glimpsed by Sexton Blake and Tinker as he went past like a petrol-driven juggernaut.

SO long as the chase led through the lighted streets of the bazaar it was not difficult for Blake to follow the dust trail, for the cloud was as plain almost as it would have been in the daytime.

But it was when Rymer should get out of the bazaar and take his way along one of the numerous roads beyond that Blake knew the real difficulty would come.

Therefore, he let his commandeered car out for all it had in it, despite the imminent risk of smashing up some of the denizens, who were scattering to right and left like panic-stricken sheep.

He couldn't guess why Rymer was in such desperate haste, but the fact itself was sufficient for Blake.

Something had happened —some crisis had arisen which had made it necessary for Rymer to seek safety at any cost. That much was plain; and, in view of what had already occurred that same evening, it was not unnatural that Blake should associate the flight with what had gone before.

Knowing as much as he did, he opined the Ligans must have some connection with it; but he little dreamed the full extent of the truth.

Rymer could not possibly know that the car coming behind at a pace which matched his own was driven by Sexton Blake.

But it would not take him long to discover that he was being pursued by some one, and Blake knew that would be quite enough to make Rymer bring into play all the dodges he knew to throw off his pursuer.

And no one had a bigger basketful of tricks than Huxton Rymer.

Some lucky star must have been in the ascendant that night, for both cars thundered out of the bazaar without any major casualties.

As they flew along Tinker noticed a smashed rickshaw, which he thought must have been struck by Rymer's mudguard, but as for themselves, they touched nothing but the road —a tribute to Blake's ability as a driver.

There were still sufficient lights about for them to follow the dust trail, and once Tinker thought he actually saw the other car just before it disappeared from view round a corner.

At any rate, the cloud of dust went that way, so Blake followed. Then, after another turn, they came into a wide, fairly straight thoroughfare, which they both recognised as one of the roads leading to the docks.

It was in better condition than the bazaar streets they had just left; and moreover, they could now see, far ahead, another car travelling at top speed.

Tinker pointed towards it and shouted something which Blake did not catch. But he had seen it too, and on they went, trying to lessen the lead which the other car was holding.

Tinker shouted again, and this time Blake caught what he said.

"He's making for the harbour!" yelled Tinker, and Blake nodded.

"Got to pick him up before he gets there!" he shouted back. "Lot of narrow streets, and might lose him among the docks!"

He was pressing the accelerator full down, and, with the cut-out open, they were making a terrific racket as they pounded along.

They passed several rickshaws and a few cars coming towards them, the occupants of which must have been amazed at the sight of the midnight race.

But a glimpse was all that was possible— a crash, a roar, the scream of the siren, and Blake and Tinker were past, their number-plate being hidden by the cloud of dust they left behind.

Then came the region of the warehouses on the right —dark, shuttered go-downs from which not a ray of light came.

And here, too, the street lamps were placed far apart, for along that broad road there is no business and little life at night.

Like a mad thing the car dashed on until Tinker saw a string of lights ahead of him.

"The harbour front!" he yelled, and Blake nodded. Then Tinker half-rose in his seat and pointed frantically to the right, for he had seen the car ahead suddenly turn in that direction.

Blake slowed down a little; and well it was for him that he did so, for as they took the corner they saw just ahead of them a car drawn full across the road, while beyond it was a burly figure racing at top speed for the nearest dock.

One second's hesitation, and Blake and Tinker would have crashed into the barricade with such terrific impact that only a miracle could have brought them out alive.

There was no room to get past the other car on either side. It was a case of trying to stop or hitting it at full speed.

Blake acted like lightning. He whipped on the brakes and gave a yell which made Tinker brace back hard.

There was a terrific grinding of outraged bands as they screamed under the friction— a wild jerk, a skid —then crash! They struck the other car full in the middle, the force of the impact and the weight of their own car almost causing a complete somersault.

For one fateful second they were poised at an angle, then over went the car on its side just as Blake and Tinker jumped clear and went rolling and scrambling through the dust. They got to their feet, spitting out grit as they staggered towards each other.

"Hurt?" asked Blake, when he could speak.

Tinker shook his head and laughed.

"Not a bit. Are you?"

"No; but I don't want to do it again. We'll have to leave the cars here for now. Come on! There he goes, down that short dock. We must get him."

To the left was a short dock, along which they could see the fugitive running. Blake and Tinker raced round the end of the car which stood across the road, and took after.

They found gates at the top of the dock, and as they reached them a Malay was just scrambling to his feet after apparently having been hurled aside by Rymer.

He went down a second time as Blake's shoulder caught him, and a stream of Malay curses followed the figure ahead.

Then suddenly the figure disappeared from view, and as they reached the edge of the dock, they saw the reason.

Lying at rest, close to the side of the dock, were a half a dozen motor-boats of various sizes. They could see Rymer jumping from one to the other, evidently trying to gain the outer craft.

Blake dropped from the edge of the dock to the nearest one, followed by Tinker, and as they sprang from boat to boat, Blake kept calling to Rymer to stop. Blake had drawn his automatic, and now Tinker followed suit. For a moment it looked as if Rymer was going to surrender, for as he heard Blake calling, he paused for a moment on the very edge of the outer boat.

Then he disappeared from view; and as Blake and Tinker dashed on, they saw the outer craft suddenly swing clear of the moorings.

Blake did not shoot. He had no intention of doing so unless Rymer started it. He wanted to get his man, but he was in no position to begin shooting promiscuously while he had so few real facts regarding the murder of Pascal and the theft of the pearls.

What he wanted was to come to grips with Rymer, and after overpowering him, force him to return to the hotel and make a statement as to what part he had played in the business.

Once he had Rymer in his power, Blake knew he would stand a pretty good chance of getting back the pearls. But, much as he wanted that, he was not prepared to go to the lengths of shooting —yet.

At the same time, with the stretch of black water growing wider and wider between the dock and the drifting boat, and Rymer struggling in the cockpit with the engine, it looked as if he might even then get away; and if he did, Blake had little doubt at the moment that the Pearls of Benjemasin would go with him.

There came a splutter and the rapid exhaust of the engine. Rymer had succeeded in starting it, and they saw him bend over and grasp the tiller. As he brought the head of the boat round he stood up and waved his hand. Then they heard his voice above the racket of the engine.

"Didn't know it was you, Blake!" he yelled. "Thought it was someone else. If you want one of the pearls, find Tom Ligan. He has it.

"I have the other, and you are welcome to it if you can get it. If you want to know who killed Pascal, find Chinaman named Kai-Wo. He's dead now, but he did it. S-o-o l-o-ong! See you in London!"

His voice died away, he waved his hand again; then he settled down beside the tiller and headed the motor-boat towards the entrance of the harbour.

Blake was standing gazing towards the fast-disappearing boat, a frown on his face.

"What about it, guv'nor?" asked Tinker, turning towards him. "We can start one of these boats and go after him."

Blake shook his head.

"We might overtake him, but we will not try to do so. We can't commandeer everything in sight. There has been enough of that already to-night. No, my lad, let him go. He may be speaking the truth when he says he has one of the pearls, and it may be true, also, that Tom Ligan has the other, though I can't figure out just how John Ligan's son comes into this thing.

"But Rymer has told us something of real value if he told the truth in saying that a Chinaman of the name of Kai-Wo killed Pascal.

"If that is so, then the Chinaman in question must be a tool of the

Ligans. After all, we are not directly interested in the pearls, although I should like to have recovered them for the sake of M. Acier.

"But the murder of Pascal is the most important thing to have cleared up. So come on! We shall return to the bazaar. I want to have a talk with Lee Sing and find out where I can locate the Ligans."

With that Blake turned and began crossing the boats towards the dock. The Malay watchman was standing waiting for them as they climbed up, but Blake merely tossed him a five-dollar note and walked on.

The man made no attempt to molest them, but on reaching the scene of the crash they found a score of Malay coolies gathered about the two cars, chattering in an excited way.

While Blake surveyed one car, Tinker examined the other. The net result was that the one which had been driven by Rymer appeared most likely to be still in condition to drive.

A few coins soon turned the gang of coolies into willing workers, and when the car which Blake had driven had been dragged aside, they made a more detailed examination of the other.

Then they climbed in, and this time Tinker took the wheel. There was a weird rattling noise as the engine started, but the gears responded to Tinker's gentle urging, and finally they got going.

Their progress back towards the bazaar was at a very different pace from that which they had made on the way to the docks.

Half a dozen times or so the engine spluttered and stopped, but Tinker was a past master at the art of coaxing a piece of machinery to obey him, and at almost a snail's pace they crept along until they came once more to the street where Lee Sing had his house and place of business.

This time there was no startling denouement to prevent them from entering the place to seek the merchant.

They found him in an upstairs room taking his ease on a low divan, while standing before him, evidently engaged in making a business report of some kind, was a brisk-looking young Chinese dressed in European clothes.

When, Blake and Tinker had made ceremonious greeting to Lee Sing, the latter indicated that the young man was his son.

Blake and Tinker were at once interested, and when the young man would have withdrawn, Blake raised his hand.

"Please remain," he said. "I have some things to say to your honourable father, and part of them concern you. But first, Lee Sing, I would ask you if you know the house which John Ligan would be likely to use as his headquarters?"

The merchant nodded.

"I know it well. But what brings you to speak of him, Mr. Blake? Have you heard that his son, Tom Ligan, was killed to-night, and that John Ligan is dying?"

"Ah!"

Blake shot a quick look at Tinker, then replied:

"I had not heard that, Lee Sing. It explains something that has been puzzling me. I must get to that house as soon as possible.

"And I shall be very grateful to you if you can provide me with a guide. Afterwards, I have some things of importance to discuss with you."

"I will not provide you with a guide, Mr. Blake, because the bazaar is in a dangerous mood to-night. Ligan's friends of a certain tong are seeking to avenge the killing.

"I have already sent patrols of the Four Lakes Tong through the bazaar to keep me informed of what is taking place. It would be unsafe for you to go to Ligan's place alone; but I, myself, will take you there. Shall we go at once?"

"I should like to do so. But tell me first, Lee Sing, have you heard anything of the murder of a European to-night?"

The old Chinaman looked at Blake for a few seconds as if debating whether to answer or not. Then he said suddenly:

"A Frenchman —yes. His body lies even now at Ligan's."

With that he rose and conducted his two European guests down the stairs. They got into Lee Sing's car, which was drawn up at the side of the street, and the merchant gave his driver instructions where to go.

As Tinker took his place beside the driver he grinned to himself, recalling how unceremoniously he had yanked the fellow out of the car when he was making his wild dash through the bazaar.

But the expressionless countenance of the Celestial revealed nothing of what he was thinking.

It was only a short drive to the house for which they were bound, but short though it was, Lee Sing had the car stopped several times while he spoke a few words to other Celestials, who seemed to appear in a most mysterious fashion from nowhere. Not until they almost reached the house did he explain.

"My men." he said briefly. "they will keep a watch on the house while we are inside in case of trouble.

"They are in greater force than Ligan's men, and I do not think there will be a fight."

When the car drew up, Lee Sing led the way into the house. The big gaming-room on the ground floor was almost deserted, and from the floor above came the sound of loud wailing.

Lee Sing ponderously began to mount the stairs, and Blake and Tinker caught sight of several heads as a score of pairs of eyes watched them from over the banisters. Then suddenly the heads disappeared and the wailing ceased. By the time they reached the top there wasn't a soul to be seen.

This didn't seem to worry Lee Sing, who appeared to know the place thoroughly. He kept on his slow and ponderous way until he came to a room on the right. Had Blake but known it, it was the same room out of which Rymer had dashed less than an hour before.

But as soon as Lee Sing pushed aside the curtain, allowing them to enter, they saw that there was indeed no doubt about the report of what had happened.

Lying on the floor, just where he had fallen, was the huddled form of Tom Ligan. In death not a hand had been lifted to do anything for him.

But John Ligan had been lifted on to a low bamboo couch, and beside him was a Chinese, who, Blake discovered later, was a herbalist. He had apparently been doing what he could for the dying man, but it was plain to the three who entered at that moment that John Ligan's moments were numbered.

He was still conscious, but showed no surprise or any particular interest in the advent of the three. Lee Sing went towards him, but Blake and Tinker bent over the huddled form of Tom Ligan.

It was not a pleasant duty Blake had to perform; but, if what Rymer had said was the truth, then there was a chance of finding one of the Pearls of Benjemasin on the person of the dead man.

And in less than half a minute he found that Rymer had not lied, for from one of the waistcoat pockets he took a tiny roll of cotton-wool, which, on being opened up, revealed one of the wonderful pearls. With it in his hand, Blake approached the couch and held it up for John Ligan to see.

"This will go to the rightful owner," he announced.

But Ligan showed no interest, and a few seconds later his eyes closed.

In the meantime, Lee Sing was in low-voiced conversation with the herbalist; and while they waited for him to finish, Blake and Tinker looked about the room trying to figure out just what had happened.

But it was Lee Sing who was to enlighten them, for from the herbalist he was getting the full details of what had taken place.

It was when they were on their way back to his place of business that he gave them the story, confirming at the same time Rymer's statement that Kai-Wo had killed Pascal.

He knew, too, in that mysterious way that things are known in Eastern bazaars, just what had happened between Rymer and the Ligans, and revealed how, after the fight with the Ligans, Rymer had had to shoot the murderer Kai-Wo in self-defence. When he had finished, Blake nodded his head.

"It all fits in with what I myself know," he remarked. "Well, Rymer got away with one of the pearls, but in meteing out the right fate to Kai-Wo, and ridding the world of two such infamous scoundrels as the two Ligans —even if it was in self-defence —I'll say that he almost deserves the pearl."

Most of which Lee Sing did not understand.

Once more in the merchant's house Blake related what had happened during his call at the Mission bungalow that evening.

From the expression in the eyes of Lee Sing's son it was plain that it is possible for a Celestial to show emotion, for he clearly revealed what he had been suffering over the uncertainty of knowing whether Sin-Len-Ye was safe or not.

And when Blake explained that Sin-Len-Ye would be very proud and happy to become the daughter of the wise and honourable Lee Sing, the young fellow grasped Tinker's hand and embarrassed the lad by the vehemence of his gratitude.

Then as it is not wise that the young men of the East should be allowed to be too much in evidence among their elders, Lee Sing dismissed his son.

They then discussed what should be done with regard to Pascal, and it was finally arranged that Blake should make a statement before the French Consul, while Lee Sing promised that he would make all arrangements for the body to be sent to the Consulate, from which the funeral would take place.

It was in the early hours of the morning when Blake and Tinker finally rose to take their departure, and as they passed out to the street, a shadowy figure came close to Tinker and pressed something into his hand.

Tinker could not be sure, but he thought it looked like Lee Sing's son. He dropped the object into his pocket, and not until they were back at the hotel did he examine it.

He gasped as he held it under the light and found that it was a gigantic yellow topaz of exquisite lustre, and obviously of rare value. It was the young lover's gratitude for what Tinker had done for little Sin-Len-Ye.

Before retiring Blake filed a second cablegram to M. Acier, detailing fully all that he had discovered, and assuring him that he, personally, would attend to all of M. Pascal's affairs.

He also reported the recovery of one of the pearl's, advising M. Acier at the same time of what had probably become of the other.

Then he and Tinker walked out on to the balcony for a final cigarette before turning in.

The next day, after arranging matters at the French Consulate (the Consul would despatch the rubies which were still in the bank to M. Acier as soon as the necessary papers came from Paris), they drove to the docks, and went back aboard the Amiral Lebon.

A good deal had happened during that brief stay ashore, and, as far as they could see, they were now finished with Rymer— for the time being, at least.

They were mistaken. The adventurer was to come into their ken far sooner than they thought, for the terrific storm which had been raging out at sea, and which struck Singapore that night, was to take a hand in the game, and the trail was to lead through queer places before they reached London.

THE END.

[26700 WORDS]

☰ The UNION JACK ☰
"SEXTON BLAKE'S OWN PAPER"

TREASURE ISLAND

The Greatest Story of Pirate Gold and Pirate
Adventure the World has Ever Known.

By Robert Louis Stevenson.

IN CASE YOU MISSED IT—and can't get back numbers.

TREASURE ISLAND!

The Greatest Story of Pirate Gold and Pirate Adventure the World has Ever Known.

By Robert Louis Stevenson.

IN CASE YOU MISSED IT —and can't get back numbers.

In the year of grace 17— there came to our inn, the Admiral Benbow, near Bristol, curious customer who was to bring a world of trouble (and adventure) to my widowed mother and me, Jim Hawkins.

He was a seafaring man, whom we came to call the Captain until we knew his real name, which was Billy Bones; but in spite of the fear into which he put our worthy neighbours of the village, he seemed to be mortal afraid of meeting any of his own kind.

Indeed, he made a bargain with me that I should "keep my weather eye open for a seafaring man with one leg."

Time went on, but it did not bring with it the one-legged seaman he feared, though after a while another of his old cronies turned up, and, though passing friends, did not receive a good reception. Indeed, the Captain chased him out of the inn with a cutlass.

Then another messenger came Old Pew, the blind beggar-man. The Captain confided to me that they were after something he had in his old sea-chest upstairs, but defied the blind man as he had done the first.

Almost as soon as Old Pew was clear of the inn, with a threat to return at ten the same night, the Captain fell dead of an apoplexy, brought on by excessive rum drinking and shock together.

My mother and I were in a quandary. There was the dead man on our parlour floor just as he had fallen, and not a soul to help us —and the villainous pirate-companions of Billy Bones due back at the inn to force him to hand over what they wanted.

Nor could we get any help from the villagers, who were in fear and trembling about meddling with the pirates' affairs. So my mother and I went back to the inn, she being set on obtaining her just dues from the Captain's money-bag.

I got the key from around his neck, and together we opened the chest. The money-bag was there right enough, but full of little except foreign gold, and my mother had a great to-do about getting the right amount, honest soul that she was. And ere she could figure it out in terms of doubloons and pieces of eight, a whistle blew outside.

The pirates, led by the blind man, were upon us!

I seized a small packet of papers from the chest to square the count, and just managed to drag my mother outside and get into hiding as the pirates swarmed along the road, entered the Admiral Benbow, and began thoroughly to ransack the place.

My mother fainted, but I could hear their shouts from where I lay. They were after something they called "Flint's Fist" —the very thing, I believed, that I had snatched from the chest at the last moment.

Then another warning whistle from along the road, where a look-out was posted, told the pirates that danger was upon them. They scattered and ran. All except Old Pew, who, blind as he was, ran right under the hoofs of a horse ridden by one of the Revenue officers coming to our assistance, and was killed.

I took my tale to good Dr. Livesey. He and the squire examined the packet I obtained —which is indeed "Flint's Fist," the chart of an island containing treasure buried by the notorious buccaneer, Captain Flint, and given by him at his death to our lodger, Billy Bones, who was his first mate.

Squire Trelawney said he would fit up an expedition to go in search of this treasure, starting from Bristol in three weeks' time. The doctor also, and me —Jim Hawkins to be cabin-boy.

In due course a ship was bought and fitted —the Hispaniola. The squire, who had been making all arrangements, wrote to say he had found a man named Long John Silver, whom he engaged as ship's cook, and who in turn recommended him to many likely looking tough old salts for the voyage.

And then I journeyed down to Bristol, ready for my great adventure. Outside a large inn I met Squire Trelawney, now dressed like a sea officer.

"Oh, sir," cried I, "when do we sail?"

"Sail!" says he. "We sail to-morrow!"

(Now go ahead with this week's gripping instalment.)

At the Sign of the Spy-Glass.

WHEN I had done breakfasting the squire gave me a note addressed to John Silver, at the sign of the Spy-glass, and told me I should easily find the place by following the line of the docks, and keeping a bright look-out for a little tavern with a large brass telescope for sign. I set off, overjoyed at this opportunity to see some more of the ships and seamen, and picked my way among a great crowd of people and carts and bales, for the dock was now at its busiest, until I found the tavern in question.

It was a bright enough little place of entertainment. The sign was newly painted; the windows had neat red curtains; the floor was cleanly sanded. There was a street on either side, and an open door on both, which made the large, low room pretty clear to see in, in spite of clouds of tobacco smoke.

The customers were mostly seafaring men, and they talked so loudly that I hung at the door, almost afraid to enter.

As I was waiting, a man came out of a side room, and, at a glance, I was sure he must be Long John. His left leg was cut off close to the hip, and under the left shoulder he carried a crutch, which he managed with wonderful dexterity, hopping about upon it like a bird. He was very tall and strong, with a face as big a ham —plain and pale, but intelligent and smiling. Indeed, he seemed in the most cheerful spirits, whistling as he moved about among the tables, with a merry word or a slap on the shoulder for the more favoured of his guests.

Now, to tell the truth, from the very first mention of Long John in Squire Trelawney's letter, I had taken a fear in my mind that he might prove to be the very one-legged sailor whom I had watched for so long at the old "Benbow." But one look at the man before me was enough. I had seen the captain, and Black Dog, and the blind man Pew, and I thought I knew what a buccaneer was like —a very different creature, according to me, from this clean and pleasant-tempered landlord.

I plucked up courage at once, crossed the threshold, and walked right up to the man where he stood, propped on his crutch, talking to a customer.

"Mr. Silver, sir?" I asked, holding out the note.

"Yes, my lad," said he; "such is my name, to be sure. And who may you be?" And then as he saw the squire's letter he seemed to me to give something like a start.

"Oh!" said he quite loud, and offering his hand, "I see. You are our new cabin-boy; pleased I am to see you."

And he took my hand in his large, firm grasp.

Just then one of the customers at the far side rose suddenly and made for the door. It was close by him, and he was out in the street in a moment. But his hurry had attracted my notice, and I recognised him at a glance. It was the tallow-faced man, wanting two fingers, who had come first to the Admiral Benbow.

"Oh," I cried, "stop him! It's Black Dog!"

"I don't care two coppers who he is," cried Silver. "But he hasn't paid his score. Harry, run and catch him."

One of the others who was nearest the door leaped up and started in pursuit.

"If he were Admiral Hawke he shall pay his score," cried Silver; and then, relinquishing my hand, "Who did you say he was?" he asked. "Black what?"

"Dog, sir," said I. "Has Mr. Trelawney not told you of the buccaneers? He was one of them."

"So?" cried Silver. "In my house! Ben, run and help Harry. One of those swabs, was he? Was that you drinking with him, Morgan? Step up here."

The man whom he called Morgan— an old, grey-haired, mahogany-faced sailor —came forward pretty sheepishly, rolling his quid.

"Now, Morgan," said Long John, very sternly, "you never clapped your eyes on that Black —Black Dog before, did you, now?"

"Not I, sir," said Morgan, with a salute.

"You didn't know his name, did you?"

"No, sir."

"By the powers, Tom Morgan, it's as good for you!" exclaimed the landlord. "If you had been mixed up with the like of that you would never have put another foot in my house, you may lay to that.

And what was he saying to you?"

"I don't rightly know, sir," answered Morgan.

"Do you call that a head on your shoulders, or a blessed dead-eye?" cried Long John. "Don't rightly know, don't you! Perhaps you don't happen to rightly know who you was speaking to, perhaps? Come now, what was he jawing —v'yages, cap'ns, ships? Pipe up! What was it?"

"We was a-talkin' of keel-hauling," answered Morgan.

"Keel-hauling, was you? and a mighty suitable thing, too, and you may lay to that. Get back to your place for a lubber, Tom."

And then, as Morgan rolled back to his seat, Silver added to me in a confidential whisper, that was very flattering, as I thought:

"He's quite an honest man, Tom Morgan, on'y stupid. And now," he ran on again, aloud, "let's see —Black Dog? No, I don't know the name, not I. Yet I kind of think I've —yes, I've seen the swab. He used to come here with a blind beggar, he used."

"That he did, you may be sure," said I "I knew that blind man, too. His name was Pew."

"It was!" cried Silver, now quite excited. "Pew! That were his name for certain. Ah, he looked a shark, he did! If we run down this Black Dog, now, there'll be news for Cap'n Trelawney! Ben's a good runner; few seamen run better than Ben. He should run him down, hand over hand, by the powers! He talked o' keel-hauling, did he? I'll keel-haul him!"

All the time he was jerking out these phrases he was stumping up and down the tavern on his crutch, slapping tables with his hand, and giving such a show of excitement as would have convinced an Old Bailey judge or a Bow Street runner. My suspicions had been thoroughly re-awakened on finding Black Dog at the Spy-glass, and I watched the cook narrowly. But he was too deep, and too ready, and too clever for me, and by the time the two men had come back out of breath, and confessed that they had lost the track in the crowd, and had been scolded like thieves, I would have gone bail for the innocence of Long John Silver.

"See here, now, Hawkins," said he, "here's a blessed hard thing on a man like me, now, ain't it? There's Cap'n Trelawney —what's he to think! Here I have this confounded son of a Dutchman sitting in my own house, drinking of my own rum! Here he comes and tells me of it plain; and here I let him give us all the slip before my blessed deadlights. Now, Hawkins, you do me justice with the cap'n. You're a lad, you are, but you're as smart as paint. I see that when you first came in. Now, here it is: What could I do, with this old timber I hobble on? When I was an A B master mariner I'd have come up alongside of him, hand over hand, and broached him to in a brace of old shakes, I would; but now —"

And then, all of a sudden, he stopped, and his jaw dropped as though he had remembered something.

"The score!" he burst out. "Three goes o' rum! Why, shiver my timbers, if I hadn't forgotten my score!"

And, falling on a bench, he laughed until the tears ran down his cheeks. I could not help joining; and we laughed together, peal after peal, until the tavern rang again.

"Why, what a precious old sea-calf I am!" he said at last, wiping his cheeks. "You and me should get on well, Hawkins, for I'll take my davy I should be rated ship's boy. But come, now, stand by to go about. This won't do. Dooty is dooty, messmates. I'll put on my old cocked hat, and step along of you to Cap'n Trelawney, and report this here affair. For, mind you, it's serious, young Hawkins; and neither you nor me's come out of it with what I should make so bold as to call credit. Nor you neither, says you; not smart —none of the pair of us smart. But dash my buttons! that was a good 'un about my score."

And he began to laugh again, and that so heartily that, though I did not see the joke as he did, I was again obliged to join in his mirth.

On our little walk along the quays he made himself the most interesting companion, telling me about the different ships that we passed by, their rig, tonnage, and nationality, explaining the work that was going forward —how one was discharging, another taking in cargo, and a third making ready for sea; and every now and then telling me some little anecdote of ships or seamen, or repeating a nautical phrase till I had learned it perfectly. I began to see that here was one of the best of possible shipmates.

When we got to the inn the squire and Dr. Livesey were seated together, finishing a quart of ale with a toast in it, before they should go aboard the schooner on a visit of inspection.

Long John told the story from first to last, with a great deal of spirit and the most perfect truth. "That was how it were, now, weren't it, Hawkins?" he would say now and again, and I could always bear him entirely out.

The two gentlemen regretted that Black Dog had got away; but we all agreed there was nothing to be done, and after he had been complimented, Long John took up his crutch and departed.

"All hands aboard by four this afternoon," shouted the squire after him.

"Ay, ay, sir," cried the cook, in the passage.

"Well, squire," said Dr. Livesey, "I don't put much faith in your discoveries as a general thing; but I will say this, John Silver suits me."

"The man's a perfect trump," declared the squire.

"And now," added the doctor, "Jim may come on board with us, may he not?"

"To be sure he may," says squire. "Take your hat, Hawkins, and we'll see the ship."

Powder and Arms.

THE Hispaniola lay some way out, and we went under the figureheads and round the sterns of many other ships, and their cables sometimes grated underneath our keel, and sometimes swung above us. At last, however, we got alongside, and were met and saluted as we stepped aboard by the mate, Mr. Arrow, a brown old sailor, with earrings in his ears and a squint. He and the squire were very thick and friendly, but I soon observed that things were not the same between Mr. Trelawney and the captain.

This last was a sharp-looking man, who seemed angry with everything on board, and was soon to tell us why, for we had hardly got down into the cabin when a sailor followed us.

"Captain Smollett, sir, axing to speak with you," said he.

"I am always at the captain's orders. Show him in," said the squire.

The captain, who was close behind his messenger, entered at once and shut the door behind him.

"Well, Captain Smollett, what have you to say? All well, I hope; all shipshape and seaworthy?"

"Well, sir," said the captain, "better speak plain, I believe, even at the risk of offence. I don't like this cruise, I don't like the men, and I don't like my officer. That's short and sweet."

"Perhaps, sir, you don't like the ship?" inquired the squire, very angry, as I could see.

"I can't speak as to that, sir, not having seen her tried," said the captain. "She seems a clever craft; more I can't say."

"Possibly, sir, you may not like your employer, either?" says the squire.

But here Dr. Livesey cut in.

"Stay a bit," said he, "stay a bit. No use of such questions as that but to produce ill-feeling. The captain has said too much or he has said too little, and I'm bound to say that I require an explanation of his words. You don't, you say, like the cruise. Now, why?"

"I was engaged, sir, on what we call sealed orders, to sail this ship for that gentleman where he should bid me," said the captain. "So far so good. But now I find that every man before the mast knows more than I do. I don't call that fair, now, do you?"

"No," said Dr. Livesey, "I don't."

"Next," said the captain, "I learn we are going after treasure — hear it from my own hands, mind you. Now, treasure is ticklish work; I don't like treasure voyages on any account; and I don't like them, above all, when they are secret, and when (begging your pardon, Mr. Trelawney) the secret has been told to the parrot."

"Silver's parrot?" asked the squire.

"It's a way of speaking," said the captain. "Blabbed, I mean. It's my belief neither of you gentlemen know what you are about; but I'll tell you my way of it —life or death, and a close run."

("Life or death, and a close run!" And so it is! The most thrilling adventures that crowd this masterly story are yet to be recorded. Don't jump an instalment and spoil the yarn. Why not place that standing order?)

!Adverisment!
SEXTON BLAKE IN SOUTH AFRICA!

Many readers have lately asked for a story of Sexton Blake in South Africa. Here it is! It will appear next week, and you will surely enjoy it. The case which took Blake to the African Veldt was in itself interesting enough, and the adventures which arose out of it were even more so. It is written by the travelled author of this week's tale. The title—

The Brand of the I.D.B.!

PAY YOUR MONEY AND TAKE YOUR CHOICE!

They're all coming soon GUNGA DASS, Mile. YVONNE, LEON KESTREL, WALDO, ZENITH THE ALBINO, HUXTON RYMER.

The UNION JACK will never be at Half-mast.

The Detective Supplement will continue as usual.

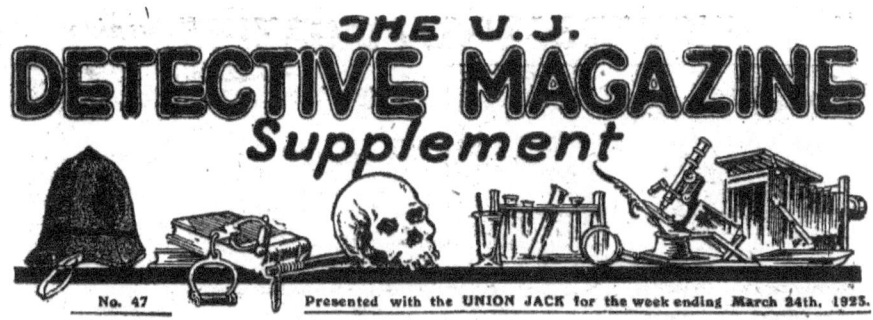

THE U.J. DETECTIVE MAGAZINE Supplement

No. 47 — Presented with the UNION JACK for the week ending March 24th, 1923.

HANDCUFFED!

By H. W. TWYMAN.

You have visualised handcuffs as a pair of iron bracelets with a chain to join them. Every detective story-writer mentions them sooner or later. Merely handcuffs. But did you happen to know that of handcuffs there are many separate and distinct varieties? All of them have their own strong points, and many have a history.

The Handcuffs shown on either side of the heading are those in use by the British Police—the "Regulation" Handcuff.

Fig. 1. Left: The "Tower and Lyon Double Lock." Centre: The Pinkerton Detective Cuff. Right: The Cobb Cuff.

HANDCUFFED!

By H. W. TWYMAN.

You have visualised handcuffs as a pair of iron bracelets with a chain to join them. Every detective story-writer mentions them sooner or later. Merely handcuffs. But did you happen to know that of handcuffs there are many separate and distinct varieties? All of them have their own strong points, and many have a history.

The Handcuffs shown on either side of the heading are those in use by the British Police —the "Regulation" Handcuff.

"THE prisoner was violent, but was handcuffed and taken to the police-station."

One often reads a sentence like that in newspapers or detective stories. We all know what handcuffs are, and pass over the word without a second thought.

Handcuffs are merely a device for locking around the wrists in order to prevent the wearer effectually using his hands.

Although there seems little scope for variety or distinction in such a commonplace contrivance, yet there are many kinds. Inventors all over the world, and during the course of generations, have exercised their ingenuity on manacles of various patterns, and there are to-day almost as many kinds of handcuffs as there are kinds of handicaps.

It is not within the scope of this short article to discuss the evolution of manacles from times long past, and, anyway, there is enough variety in the way of modern handcuffs to catalogue.

We need only pause in passing to imagine the ponderous chains and fetters that kept prisoners securely captive in the dark and noisome dungeons far beneath the olden Tower of London's moat.

No mere bracelets these; they were substantial enough to tether a mammoth, bolted into the solid masonry at one end, and riveted about the unlucky captive's limbs at the other.

Often enough there was a huge iron ball attached to the leg-irons to prevent any tendency towards friskiness, should the prisoner have had any feelings that way.

The curious may still behold specimens of such gruesome relics in the Tower of London itself, where they are displayed as museum pieces amongst other survivals from a bygone age, and serve to remind us that we live in happier times.

Irons and manacles in the past were not designed for comfort or convenience, or even lightness.

When the powers got their hands on a "wanted" man in those days they meant to keep him. They fitted him snugly into an outfit of chains whose weight made him sag at the knees, and, in case the anklets and wrist-pieces might shake loose, riveted them into position.

Then, as already hinted, they would probably fasten the whole lot to a heavy ring-bolt embedded in the stone wall.

Once in his dungeon, the prisoner was likely to remain there.

There seems to be no outstanding record of escapes from old-time fortresses under these conditions, and Houdinis of those days were stopped at the start.

Even as late as the time of the Bow Street runners[1] they still believed in weight for handcuffs. A notorious bank-robber named Mackcoull was sent from London to Scotland with the "bracelets" on.

But they must have been cumbrous bracelets, for they weighed forty pounds, and probably prevented their wearer turning any handsprings on the journey, too.

In these enlightened times we have progressed a good way on the road to humanity in the matter of handcuffs.

It was only last March that a distinguished judge at the Old Bailey —Judge Atherley Jones —protested in court against the type of handcuffs that were in use by the officers at Scotland Yard.

They were an American pattern, and worked on the ratchet principle, as illustrated.

Evidence had been given that the handcuffs in question became so tight that it took more than an hour to release the prisoner. The judge asked for the cuffs to be produced, and gave them a prolonged scrutiny.

His opinion was decidedly against them.

"It is highly discreditable that they should be used in this country," he said. "We do not want to go back to the days of thumbscrews."

The peculiarity of this type of bracelet is that, the more the wearer struggles to free himself from them the tighter they become. Being adjustable, they can be arranged so as to fit the largest or the smallest wrist, and, once fitted, can only be removed by means of the right key.

A "handcuff king" who did not have a very high opinion as to their restraining capabilities—or who had a very high opinion of his own cleverness —once entered a shop in the Strand in which they are sold and accepted a challenge to free himself from a pair of these ratchet handcuffs.

They were put on, and he began to make good his challenge.

But the cuffs would not cooperate. They resisted for more than an hour, and the handcuff king; very red in the face, and breathing heavily, at last had to confess himself beaten.

---

[1] The Bow Street Runners have been called London's first professional police force. The force originally numbered six men and was founded in 1749 /drf; Wiki

But to go back to the judge.

After his protest from the bench, Judge Atherley Jones was interviewed by a newspaper man and asked to elaborate his views.

He repeated his former opinion, and added that his ideas were shared by people most competent to judge the matter.

"The mischief of these handcuffs," he said, "is that, if the constable who puts them on is not very careful, he may fasten them too tightly on the prisoner's wrists. The operation, therefore, depends on the humanity or otherwise of the constable.

"Moreover, as the handcuffs work on cogs or teeth, if the prisoner knocks them against any unyielding surface he will tighten them still more, and they may cut into his flesh.

The then Home Secretary, Mr. Shortt, differed, however.

"The handcuffs are less likely to injure prisoners than the old pattern," he remarked. "No other complaints have been received, and it is evident that the judge has never seen them, because his description of them is hopelessly inaccurate."

The judge, however, maintained that they had been demonstrated to him by a police-inspector.

Whatever the real facts, and however opinions may vary, it seems pretty certain that these ratchet handcuffs do remain on a man's wrists till they are officially removed.

It is not certain what was the make of the pair actually under discussion, but there are several kinds of these toothed cuffs, and they all come from America.

The accompanying illustration (Fig. 1) shows three of them, each differing slightly, and each known by its distinctive name.

That on the left is known as the "Tower and Lyon Double Lock," the right-hand pair is the "Cobb 1900," and the one in the centre is the "Pinkerton Detective Cuff."

The latter appears to be merely a name, however, for it does not appear that this kind of manacle was ever used by the great American detective.

To better illustrate the working principle of a ratchet handcuff, an illustration of the mechanism is given on page 301.

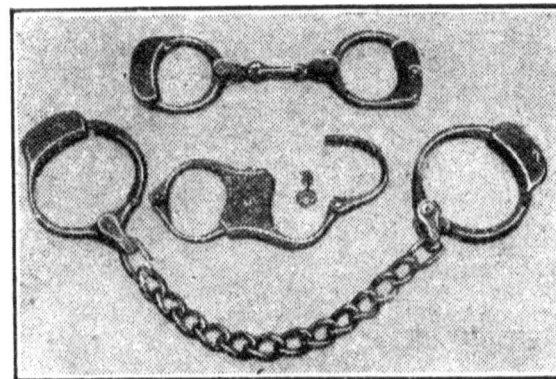

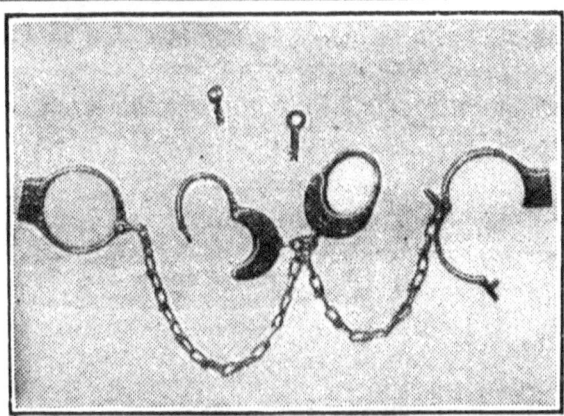

Fig. 3. The Rankin leg-iron and handcuff combination.

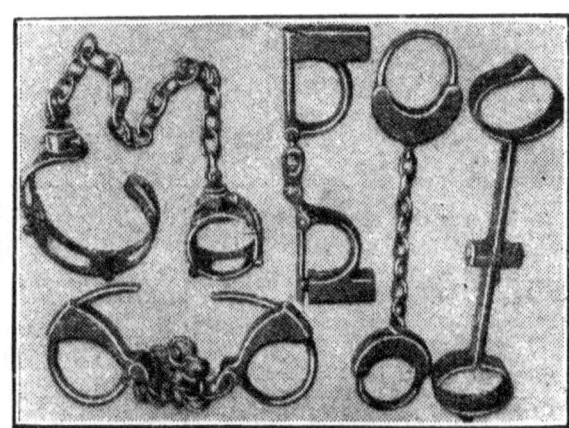

An example of ratchet-worked leg-irons, used in American prisons, is shown in Fig. 4, in the left-hand bottom corner.

America has also produced several other varieties of handcuff.

There are, for instance, the inventions of Captain E. D. Bean, of Boston, three specimens of which are illustrated in Fig. 2. The topmost one in the photograph is the type of handcuff used in prisons, and the centre cuff, without a central chain, is known as the "Bean Giant."

A man wearing this contrivance is forced to carry his hands absolutely rigid and independently immovable; even the small freedom of a link or two is denied him—a precaution that is sometimes necessary in the cases of desperate or homicidal prisoners.

The manacles at the bottom are leg-irons, also fitted with the special Bean lock.

There is also another formidable American manacle known as the Rankin Combination, pictured in Fig. 3. In this case the handcuffs and the leg-irons are fastened together, and all the four locks are secured in different ways, and require a special key to each.

In the American Civil War an astonishingly great use was made of handcuffs for the many deserters who were captured. In this case a rather unusual bracelet was used.

Instead of the normal flexible chain, each cuff was held rigidly in position by means of a thick bar of metal. The locking arrangement was exceptionally easy to snap shut, but equally difficult to unfasten. Indeed, it was found impossible in many cases, and during the course of the war hundreds of them had to be filed and sawn off the prisoners' wrists.

They came to be known as "Bounty Jumpers," these manacles, from the fact that they were used on men who had enlisted in the Army for the sake of the bounty that was given, and then ran away to join again.

A very similar handcuff to this, but of modern manufacture, is known as the "Lilly Iron," a picture of which appears on the right-hand side of Fig. 4. As a study in contrasts, the much more humane cuffs shown on the left of the same picture represent those in use by the American Army of to-day. Although probably as just as serviceable, they are altogether lighter and much less irksome.

The Lilly Lion was named after its inventor, Captain Lilly, of the United States Army, who, strangely enough, died with a pair of them on him, although in what circumstances it is not certain.

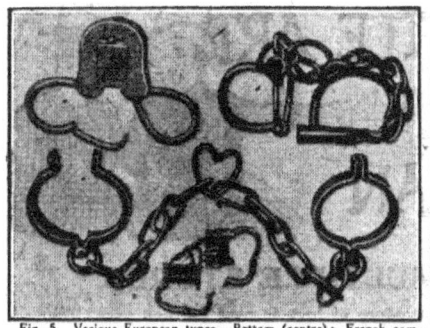

Fig. 5. Various European types. Bottom (centre): French combination letter handcuff. Centre: Russian leg-irons. The heart-shaped link denotes that the wearer is a murderer and a life-termer. Note the absence of locking arrangements. These leg-irons are riveted on for life.

Fig. 8. An adaptation of the ratchet type favoured by the German police. This is known as the Stotz Handcuff.

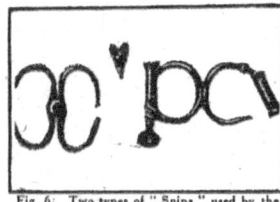

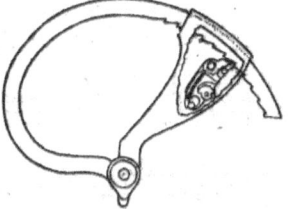

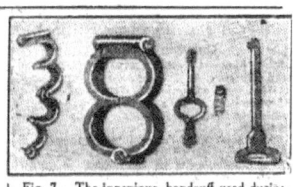

Fig. 7. The ingenious handcuff used during the South African War on deserters. This type is known as the Plug 8.

Fig. 6. Two types of "Snips" used by the British police.

Diagram illustrating the mechanism of a typical American ratchet handcuff. Note the teeth, which allow the hinged portion to move inwards but not outwards.

The manacles which appear in the centre of the same photo —the pair with the square, cumbrous locks —are specially interesting on account of their having been first worn by the murderer of the American President Garfield. The assassin's name was Guiteau, and the cuffs are accordingly known as the "Guiteau Cuff."

They are of extraordinarily heavy design, and the locks which secure them are both complicated and efficient. A specially contrived double key is required to unfasten them.

Quite a different type of handcuff is one which is extensively used in France. The locks in this type are somewhat on the lines of a bank safe combination lock. There is no key required, except a memorised word.

As will be seen by a glance at the bottom of Fig. 5, each cuff carries a drum-like arrangement of revolving discs. These are marked with letters, and the discs have to be turned until the letters stand in their proper sequence, when —and only when —the cuff can be opened.

This method is rather complicated in working, but the lock is correspondingly secure.

Each country, of course, has its favoured type quite distinct from others, though all bear a family resemblance.

Germany, for instance, uses a ratchet pattern something like the American, while those in common use by our English police have a distinct shape all their own. The German type is known as the "Stotz Cuff" (Fig. 8).

As may be imagined, Russia— especially in the days of Czardom and indiscriminate imprisonment —has a mediaeval taste in irons.

Their brightest effort in this direction was in the case of murderers. Their handcuffs and leg-irons were not locked on, but riveted.

The manacles were made to do double duty, for, in addition to restricting the prisoner, they also indicated what his crime was. The central link of the chain was fashioned in various ways to denote the crime committed and the length of time the wearer was serving. A heart indicated that the prisoner was a murderer and a "lifer," and lesser crimes were shown by a spade, a club, or a diamond.

This is clearly demonstrated in Fig. 5. Note also the absence of any locking arrangement, and the portions bent up at the end for riveting purposes.

Truly an unbecoming lifelong ornament!

Our own police use handcuffs only when they have to. In fact, there are the most stringent rules laid down on the subject, and any constable who infringes them will soon find himself in trouble.

Hear what the official "Police Code" has to say about it:

"Handcuffs should not be used except in cases of necessity — when a prisoner is violent and likely to attempt to escape, or if the number of prisoners to be conveyed, or the special circumstances render such a precaution necessary to prevent a rescue, or the prisoner doing injury to himself.

"In conveying a prisoner, prior to conviction, by rail or otherwise, handcuffing must necessarily depend on whether he is likely to attempt to escape, and whether his doing so would be likely to succeed, by reason of his superior strength, or by the fatigue of the officer, as also on the nature of his offence.

"Persons in custody for crimes of violence may well be handcuffed, while those apprehended for perjury and like offences should be treated somewhat differently.

"If handcuffs are unnecessarily put on and the prisoner is

acquitted, he might bring an action and recover damages against the officer."

With this official warning ringing in his ears, it is obvious that a British police-constable would think twice before using the "darbies" without good cause.

The commonest English pattern of handcuff, or "Regulation" cuff, as it is sometimes called, is of the snap variety. That is, it requires no locking up, but is fastened by mere pressure and snapped into place. It is opened by means of a curiously-shaped key, which is inserted in the end of the thicker part of the cuff and twisted round.

A lesser known variety are known as "Snips," or "Twisters." They are similar in form to the Regulation pattern, except that they have no central connecting-links, but are joined in the middle. These are shown in Fig. 6.

The object of these is to exert persuasion on a very unruly prisoner who will not "come quietly."

The constable can make his capture walk along as sedately as a boarding-school miss merely by giving the cuff a twist, and thus exerting painful, pressure on the prisoner's forearm.

Not the least ingenious handcuff ever invented —and then the present list is done— was one which was used a great deal in the South African War. (Fig. 7.)

When closed, this manacle resembles a figure "8," and is made in two pieces, hinged at one end. It embodies a novel locking device.

When the cuffs are placed in position and locked, a steel plug is pushed into the keyhole, which is circular. To get this plug out again, it is necessary to use a suitable key (also shown). This key has two specially shaped teeth at one end, which engage in the holes of the plug, and, if operated the right way, unscrew it.

Then, but not until the plug has been removed, the key can be turned round and the other end used to unfasten the lock.

From its shape and its special feature, this unique bracelet is known as the "Plug 8." It is a product of Birmingham.

LAUGHTER IN COURT!

A few of the unintentionally funny things Magistrates have to listen to.

Magistrate: "What is the trouble in the house?"
Witness: "Three women and one bathroom."
*   *   *

"Does your husband like work?" asked the judge.
"He is a lover of it," replied the wife. "Even when he cannot get it."
*   *   *

At Bow County Court:
"Yes," replied the witness. "She gets a few jobs now and again."
"And what do you do?"
"Me do? Why, nothin'. I'm drawing the dole."
*   *   *

"Is it correct that your husband is a notorious blackguard?" asked a solicitor.
"Well," replied the wife, "he is the best I could make of him out of the raw material."

At Marylebone County Court:
"Whom were you with at the time?"
"A lady friend and her bloke."
* * *

"What sort of a woman is your wife?"
"She's no oil painting," replied her better half, "but she's quiet in harness, and that's how you want 'em."

"And what effect did the assault have on you?"
"Ever since she threw the bowl of water over me I've been in an unsprung condition."
Judge: "Unstrung, I suppose you mean?"
*   *   *

Solicitor: "Have you a bath-room in your flat?"
Wife: "No; my husband would be ashamed to have a bath."
*   *   *

A man applied at Edmonton County Court for a summons against his lodger.

"What is the trouble between you?" asked the judge.

"Why," explained the landlord, "when I wanted to put my kettle on to boil, my lodger sat down on the stove and stopped me."

THE GENTLE ART OF THE 'CON' MAN

THE TALE OF THE MULTIPLE STORES.

The game of the confidence man, like the story of love, is ever old and ever new. Every fresh business success brings in its train a whole host of new confidence wheezes, and every wheeze finds victims. The latest activities of these silver-tongued gentry concerns a shopkeeper's fear of competition which did not exist—and his subsequent loss of good hard cash.

" Your goods don't compare with ours, do they ? " ventured the salesman. The shopkeeper admitted the grave impeachment and a silence heavy with hesitations followed.

The Gentle Art of the 'Con'man
THE TALE OF THE MULTIPLE STORES.

The game of the confidence man, like the story of love, is ever old and ever new. Every fresh business success brings in its train a whole host of new confidence wheezes, and every wheeze finds victims. The latest activities of these silver-tongued gentry concerns a shopkeeper's fear of competition which did not exist —and his subsequent loss of good hard cash.

WHENEVER there is a new business success, there is a new confidence game.

Let men in California find gold in the beds of the creeks and the country is soon offered the finest hand-plated gold bricks, the most charmingly engraved shares in non existent if otherwise praiseworthy mines, and the most alluring if slightly barren opportunities in yellow

94

if not gold bearing ores.

Let some one eke a bit of money out of mineral oils, and what a deluge of oily promoters sells a whole generation of our people blocks of stock in oil-less wells!

Or let some one turn a few millions out of the chug and rattle of a motor, and witness the endless procession of motor promotions dealing in engines that never operated and cars that never ran, alas!

Every discovery, every invention, every strike of natural wealthy and every land promotion, triumphant speculation, noteworthy commercial organisation, or spectacular accession of wealth, no matter what its character, has its camp followers of con men with their games which are, like the story of love, ever old and ever fresh.

Opening a Shop.

So it happens that twenty or thirty men were arrested in Pittsburg the other day on the seemingly absurd charge of having attempted to open a grocery shop —a circumstance which requires elaborate explanation.

To understand this curious circumstance fully, it is essential to take a cursory view of the development of the American retail business, and its trend toward what some call "trust formation" and others "centralisation."

Fifty years ago the merchandise staples of the country were distributed entirely by small general shops in the small towns, villages, and hamlets, which were then the buying and selling centres for the great bulk of our population.

Your shopkeeper handled everything from a grand piano or a farm wagon to a paper of pins, and the farmer and townsman came to him for goods and carted them home himself.

It was a comfortable, lazy, wasteful, and generally inefficient method, but it gave a lot of persons something to do that was remunerative and independent,

A Commercial War.

Along came the mail-order houses, which brought in huge allotments, waged their selling campaigns through the economical mails, sold a great deal cheaper than the small local merchant, and soon closed the doors of many a tradesman.

The small fish of the mercantile seas could not drive out these whales; but it happens that there are many lines or goods which cannot be sold advantageously through the post, and in these the little local merchant continued to deal profitably.

But as far back as thirty years ago the movement began to centralise even these lines, and there sprang up the group of multiple shops, small enterprises at first, according to the measure of these days, but constantly growing in numbers, size, and power.

First came little strings of shops dealing in the staples of the grocery line, the so-called tea and coffee stores, later organised into several great combines.

Then followed chain cigar stores, chain chemist shops, chain sweet shops, hat shops, shoe shops, and what not.

Spectacular Success.

From the rise of these organisations or shops sprang two states of mind, one affecting the small merchants of every town, and one acting upon the public generally.

Many of these combines were spectacular successes. Their founders rose to enormous wealth, and their stocks, reached high levels of value on the exchanges, so that the great class of Americans whose members are eternally looking for the chance to get rich without labour were fired and enthused.

Thus, the notion of speculating in chain-shop shares was put into many thousands of otherwise rather over-vacant heads.

The other state of mind grew from an exaggerated form of the fear and wrath which the mail-order houses originally engendered in the brains of local merchants.

Not a small grocer or druggist or general merchant who did not live in daily dread and nightly sweat for fright of the multiple shop's coming!

Here was an enemy that could not be fought, a competition that could not be met, a peril that could only be prayed against.

So the ground was prepared for one of the most deadly effective con games ever perpetrated in America. Hence the men in Pittsburg were arrested. Let us see how and why.

Back in 1902, just twenty years ago, Mr. Samuel Parkinson went out to Somewhere, Pennsylvania, with a little money he had inherited from his Aunt Suzanne, and opened a first-class grocery shop.

There were five other grocers in the little town at the time, but Sam had looked them over, weighed them in his business balance, and found them wanting.

He had the idea that a hustling young person like himself could beat the lot of them, and so he invested and went to work.

The Rise of Samuel Parkinson.

And he prospered.

In 1908 he had bought the two-story frame building which harboured his grocery, becoming a taxpayer and incipient magnate.

In 1909 he had been nominated for the city council and received some votes, albeit not enough.

The following year he had married the wry-necked daughter of Banker O'Malley, and thereafter he had ruled the roost so far as groceries, and lofty prices, were concerned.

He had the other grocers pretty well beaten, and was running toward fortune and ease.

He was a social, and business figure in the town, a member in good voice of all the local clubs, a regular attendant of the right church, officer of all the approved lodges.

That was the state of affairs with Samuel Parkinson on an evening late last spring, just before a stranger came into Somewhere, in a shiny motor-car and something exploded in Sam's little world.

The gentleman in the motor had come to establish a multiple shop, and, what was worse, he broke the dreadful news to Sam Parkinson first and foremost of all.

He was pleasant about it, this unctuous stranger. He bore Sam not the slightest of all slight ill wills, but business was business.

Ergo, that shop would have to be opened, much as it might pain some persons. However, if Mr. Parkinson was willing, the stranger would like to drop around in a day or two and talk things over.

Parkinson is Depressed.

Perhaps they might come to an understanding. There might be a way of operating to their mutual advantage. Satisfactory?

The stranger said his name was Summers, and that he represented the Allied Chain Stores Ltd. Having revealed so much, he went upon his way.

Sam Parkinson went home to his wife in no balmy mood. He knew well enough what was going to happen. This rapacious trust, this heartless combine, was coming into his town to throttle honest individual enterprise.

It would rent the best corner in the town, open a shop that would make his look like a barn, sell inferior goods at lower rates, cut prices, run continual sales, advertise, attract crowds, and force the pace all the way round.

Sam would have to keep up with this energetic selling or sell out. He would have to spend money and effort. He would have to sell twice as much to make the same profit. All the cream was about to be skimmed from his milk.

And, worse yet, he was going to have to get up and move.

The Lure of the Penny.

His wife, who was something of a local busybody on her own account, tried to reassure the worried grocer.

After all, she would see that the right people continued to trade with him and had nothing to do with this interloping trust.

She might be relied upon to keep the ladies of the Benevolent Society and others solidly in line for Sam and the good old order.

But Sam shook his head dolefully. He knew that a difference of one penny in the price of a bushel of potatoes would make more difference in the end to the housewives of Somewhere than all the clubs and orders on the map.

He cast a jaundiced eye upon the past and recited to his wife the triumphs of the multiple shops and the ever-diminishing line of small shopkeepers.

Say what she might, the coming of the trust was a disaster to them, and one not to be disguised. In this mood Sam went to a sleepless bed.

Late the following morning the unhappy grocer was putting up an order for a woman customer when the resplendent person of Mr. Summers appeared in his doorway.

Mr. Summers perched himself on a case of prunes and waited for the attention of the merchant.

Nor did Sam waste much time getting round to this interesting and sinister caller. They found a quiet corner, and Mr. Summers began.

A Fatherly Combine.

First of all, he said, the shopkeepers of the country had a very wrong impression of the multiple shop companies or, at least, of the Allied.

It seemed to be the impression of local merchants that the Allied was a trade octopus, reaching out its slimy tentacles to clutch and throttle the small man in the little towns.

But nothing was further from the truth, nothing more desperately unjust and false. The Allied was, in fact, the friend and patron of the small merchant.

It aimed to befriend and not to destroy the local dealer. Instead of crowding him out, it intended always to benefit him and make use of his acquaintance, influence, and support.

"What?" ejaculated the startled Mr. Parkinson.

"Pree-cise-ly," echoed Mr. Summers. "If you think I've come here to put you out of business, Mr. Parkinson, you've got me and the Allied all wrong.

"We're here to help you and ourselves at the same time. If you aren't too busy, I'd like to show you a picture of Old Man Opportunity in his best Sunday dress."

Whereupon Mr. Summers dug down into a case he carried and proceeded to bring forth a line of samples —bottles, cans, jars, cartons, cakes, boxes, packages, packets, and rolls.

One by one he held them up for the view and approval of the grocer, asking all the while whether the lines carried by Sam were any better than these, or half so good.

And Sam, looking, turning, twisting, tasting, and sniffling, was forced to admit that the goods he was buying through the regular trade were nowise superior to these samples.

Introducing Father Opportunity.

"I should say not." Mr. Summers agreed. "We are not like so many of the multiple shop groups, a combination of cheapjack shops.

"We aim to give quality at a low price. By means of co-operative buying and, in most instances, the operation of our own manufactories, we are able to put out standard goods at prices to compete with second-class wares. That's where old Opportunity hides."

Summers dug down into his portfolio and produced an imposing list of prices, everything from one end of the alphabet to the other in almost endless variety.

"How much did you pay for these prunes I'm sitting on?" he asked suddenly.

Sam told him.

"No better and no worse than the average, eh?" asked Summers.

"I guess so," Sam was forced to agree.

"Well, how do you like our price on the same goods?" demanded Summers, poking the price-list under the grocer's nose.

For the rest of the week Sam led the eloquent Summers about his town from one moneyed man to another. Unknowingly he was but leading other sheep to the slaughter.

Mr. Parkinson's Falling Heart.

Sam began to study this chart of prices with rising interest and a falling sensation about the heart.

Everything on the list was quoted at figures considerably lower than any he could get from his jobbers.

It was certain he could never compete with a store that was getting goods at such rates.

Summers started to walk round the place inspecting the goods, stating their prices with the accuracy of one thoroughly conversant with groceries, and comparing these rates with his own listings.

Then he came back and sat down again with the discomfited and harried grocer.

"Well," ventured the salesman, "no comparison at all, is there?"

Sam admitted the grave impeachment, and there was a silence heavy with hesitations.

"Mr. Parkinson," the redoubtable Summers began, in his best oratorical tone, "how would you like to get this line of goods at these prices and go up against the other merchants of this town with such an advantage? You'd do some business, eh?"

"I would," said Sam succinctly.

"Well, Mr. Parkinson," said the radiant Summers, "that's the opportunity I've come to offer you if you're the right man.

"How'd you like to be the independent representative of the

Allied Chain Stores in this here splendid town?"

Fulsome Flattery.

But Sam was too full for utterance, so Summers went ahead.

He had been around, looked the ground over, made cautious inquiries, and studied the locality.

He had determined that Sam was the leading merchant in his line, that he enjoyed an enviable reputation, that his connections were the best and his standing the most secure.

To be sure, Summers had also looked up the standing of Jim Jones, the grocer in the next street.

He had discovered that Jones, too, was a man of substance and reputation. As a matter of fact, he liked Jones' position and shop a little better than Sam's.

Again, Jones had always been more of a popular-priced grocer. For a long time, Summers admitted, he had been in a quandary, but at length he had decided to give Sam the first chance.

If he didn't want to play, there was still time to offer the same proposition to Brother Jones.

At the very suggestion, Sam Parkinson was frozen wordless. He tried to grasp the fleeting opportunity. He tried to talk, to protest, to cry out, but it was of no use.

Before he could utter a sound, Summers was talking again.

Dinner for Two.

"You think about it a while," he said. "Then I'd like you to come and have dinner with me at the hotel, where we can talk things over right.

"How'll six o'clock suit you? All right? Well, good-bye. See you at six."

And without more ado the man was gone. Moreover, he was off in the direction of Jones' shop, a fact which gave our friend Samuel a most distressing afternoon.

At six o'clock Sam Parkinson found a table laid for two in the quietest corner of the hotel's dining-room.

Here he sat down with the genial Summers, who immediately decanted something from a pocket-flask, assured Sam that it was from his private cellar in New York, and urged him to drink without fear or restraint.

Thus fortified, Sam let himself in for the best dinner the hotel could provide, and Summers kept urging him to go the limit and let the joy of the occasion be unconfined.

When the last sip of coffee was gone, he produced long, black cigars which, looked their value, urged one upon Sam, and leaned back in his chair to talk.

Local Faults.

Mr. Summers reviewed the troubles and faults of local shopkeeping as one having intimate knowledge.

In the first place, the small, local dealer could not buy in quantities and still keep up the freshness of his wares.

He was compelled to buy little dribs and drabs, and Sam knew well what the jobbers were in the habit of doing on small orders.

Again, the retail merchant was up against a wholesaler's trust. No one could know better than Sam that there was no competition among wholesalers. Let any man go out and try to buy a case of tinned foods of a certain quality.

He would find that one wholesaler charged exactly the same as all others. Here was a combination in restraint of trade and in violation of the retailer's interest, but what was to be done?

And back of this stood the packers' and manufacturers' combinations. What chance was there for the retailer when these great organisations had long since got together and fixed their prices on a non-competitive basis?

Obviously, there was only one salvation, and that was a combination of small merchants, by means of which the wholesaler and the manufacturer could be fought and beaten.

That was what the Allied Retail Stores was and did. By joining the ranks, Sam would become his own wholesaler, packer, and manufacturer.

It was his one chance to beat off the enemies that had him and all his brethren by the throats.

Competition.

"We are, as you know, our own wholesalers," said Summers. "We are quantity buyers of everything that goes into the grocery line, for we shall have to supply a chain of at least two to three hundred stores in this section of the country.

"We already have more than a hundred in our membership, and we are recruiting new ones every day.

"But we are much more than wholesalers. We are also our own packers, manufacturers, and in some instance our own producers.

"We cut out the middleman all along the line and supply our various branch stores with our goods at the lowest possible figures.

"We are prepared to compete with anybody in the business and go them all one better. How's that for an idea?"

Sam Parkinson had to agree that it was not a notion to be sneezed at, but he wondered just how far it would aid him.

"Good Lord, man!" ejaculated the seemingly impatient Summers. "You don't seem to grasp the idea. Don't you understand that if you join the Allied you participate in the wholesalers' profits and the manufacturers' profits and the producers' profits in everything the combine takes in?

"What do you think I mean when I say this is a mutual profit-sharing proposition? Let me explain the whole thing once more."

Pressing the Point.

"You join the Allied Stores, and put in our lines of goods at the prices on the list. With them on your shelves, you run your shop just as you always did.

"It remains yours, and not ours. The only difference is that, because you handle our goods, and are a member of our chain, you get extra accommodations in the way of credit, you get the benefit of our advertising, and the advantage of our constant deliveries in fresh goods.

"We have already taken an option on a great warehouse in Pittsburg, and I'll gladly show you the bills of lading for trainloads of goods which are coming to fill it.

"From that convenient point you'll be supplied daily, if necessary.

"But that's only half of it. As producers, we charge ourselves with a producer's profit. As manufacturers, we take off a manufacturer's bit, and we also take down a wholesaler's profit.

"All this happens before the goods reach you, and these various profits are included in the price you pay as retailer.

"Now, these various profits that pile up have to be divided somehow, don't they? They must go to someone, mustn't they?

"Well, they go to the members of the Allied Chain Stores. That means, to you and the other merchants who have joined the chain and own its stock."

Stock Shy.

"Oh. I'm to take stock, am I?" asked Mr. Parkinson, believing that he had found the flaw, and recoiling with a proper reserve.

"That's up to you," said Summers. "If you don't, someone else will."

Mr. Parkinson considered the threat of this assertion with solemn and painful attention.

He had heard that stocks were bad things to buy. Indeed, he had sunk a good bit of hard money into an oil venture some years before, been denuded of his money, and then been soundly laughed at by his banker father-in-law, with the result that he had taken a vow against all stocks whatsoever.

If it was a stock proposition, he wasn't interested, and he said as much.

Summers now launched into his real arguments and persuasions. He made it clear that an organisation of this kind could only operate by means of large cash capital.

There were two ways of getting it. One would be to go to the capitalists, in which case they would expect to take the profits, leaving the retailer no better off than he was in the beginning.

The other method was to get the capital for the manufacturing and distributing features of the business from the retailers, thereby keeping the control of the business in their hands, and turning back to them the complete profits of the entire enterprise.

Springing the Hurrah!

Certainly this was a clear and reasonable proposition. Any man in the grocery business could see what it meant.

However, if Mr. Parkinson wasn't interested, it was always possible to go to Jones. Very likely he would view the matter in a more reasonable light.

So the wily Summers kept playing alternately upon the reason, the greed, the fear, and the envy of the local merchant.

Parkinson could not let the proposition get out of his hands and into those of his rival. Neither could he persuade himself to get away from his prejudice against stocks.

Here Summers came with the "hurrah!" on him —that piece of dramatics that marks the climax of every confidence game.

"Mr. Parkinson, you haven't got the whole plan before you yet," he said. "You are one of those men who have lost money on stock speculations, with the result that you have a prejudice.

"But there is as much difference in stocks as there is in canned peaches. You probably bought stock before in a business you knew nothing about.

"This time you're asked to invest in your own business, Mr. Parkinson—your very own business.

"You're simply asked to use our capital for the expansion of your own trade and the increase of your own profits.

"That's what every business man does with his money. Just because you've got the word 'stock' caught in your mind, you misapprehend the whole idea.

"You don't even let me explain how small your allotment of stock will be, and you haven't yet let me tell you the greatest feature of our whole plan."

Sam Parkinson was at least willing to listen, and Summers went on to explain.

Splitting the Stock.

The Allied company had set aside two thousand pounds' worth of stock to be subscribed in the city of Somewhere, he said.

This total was based upon computations which took into consideration the population of the town and the volume of grocery business done there.

Smaller places would be asked to subscribe for only half as much, and larger communities would have to take twice or three times as much if they were to have the benefits of an Allied store.

No, no, no, no! Sam Parkinson was not expected to take two thousand pounds' worth of stock. The Allied people knew he had no such amounts of cash available.

Wouldn't he please listen, and learn what the scheme was? Very well.

The city of Somewhere was to take two thousand pounds in stock. Of this amount Sam was to take two hundred, or even three hundred pounds' worth.

The rest was to be taken by the other people of the town who wanted to make some easy money. No doubt Sam knew enough moneyed men to take over the allotment without much trouble.

And what were the benefits to Sam? Just think! If Sam got ten or twenty of his best customers and richest acquaintances to take stock in the Allied stores, where would these people do their trading?

Naturally, they would come to the Allied stores for everything they needed, since their patronage helped to pay the dividends in which they would participate.

At the same time, Sam would take the whole retail profit from this augmented business for himself.

Was that fair? Was that a noble idea? Had anybody ever invented a more effective manner of tying up customers to a store and forcing people to deal exclusively with one merchant?

Now what had Mr. Parkinson to say? Was it still a stock-jobbing proposition? Had he any further hesitancy?

Let him think what was being offered in return for his small subscription and his influence in selling the rest of the local allotment.

Points in the Scheme.

First of all, he got his goods at greatly reduced prices.

Second, he would always have credit with the Allied stores for double the amount of his personal stock subscription.

Third, he would participate in the manufacturer's and distributor's profits to the extent of his share holding.

And, fourth, he would compel the leading people of the town to trade with him permanently and exclusively out of self-interest.

Mr. Summers pushed back his chair and rose.

"Think it over till to-morrow," he said. "I'll have to ask you for some kind of answer in the morning, because I've promised to let Jones know where I stand in the afternoon.

"He's heard about the proposition, and is wild to get aboard."

Saying so, Summers went up to his room, and Sam Parkinson wandered home, thrilling and thinking. It really was a wonderful plan.

For the rest of the week Sam Parkinson led the eloquent Summers about his town, from one moneyed man to the other, introducing the promoter and explaining the wonders and merits of the Allied stores plan.

Summers was, of course, playing an old game on the innocent city of Somewhere.

A leading business man is picked out and induced to take stock by fair means or foul.

He is then used to lead the other sheep to the slaughter, and they follow their leader blindly into the killing pens.

So with the people of Somewhere, including the good banking father-in-law of Sam, who had laughed so raucously about his relative's oil stock.

Exit Mr. Summers

Within ten days Mr. Summers had disposed of his allotment of stock. Having done so, he purred away in his motor-car, taking with him some cash and several large certified cheques.

So far as Sam Parkinson and the good people of Somewhere are concerned, that was the end of the chapter.

No goods ever came to Sam's store, no dividends were ever paid, and no Allied stores blossomed out in all the many communities where they had been promised.

Nothing happened at all, except that Somewhere soon awoke to the realisation that a confidence man had got two thousand pounds, which amount Sam Parkinson has promised to repay when his ship comes in.

In the course of the last winter and spring more than two hundred small cities and towns in the south and central West have been victimised in this manner through the operations of a single well-organised gang, whose leaders the writer knows by name and record.

More than thirty salesmen of the kind typified by Mr. Summers have been working these towns.

Most of them were in the crowd arrested in Pittsburg the other day.

The significance of these arrests lies in the fact that this was the first occasion upon which the multiple shop game has been brought into a large city.

Heretofore the swindlers have contented themselves with the country towns, where police protection is supposed to be less efficient and the merchants less sophisticated.

But the invasion of the cities having been undertaken, we shall shortly see the retail merchants of New York and Chicago succumb to some variation of this game, just as their country cousins have been doing for the last year.

Verily, every business has its con game.